demon envy

demon envy

ERIN LYNN

BERKLEY JAM, NEW YORK

THE BERKLEY PUBLISHING GROUP
Published by the Penguin Group
Penguin Group (USA) Inc.
375 Hudson Street, New York, New York 10014, USA

Penguin Group (Canada), 90 Eglinton Avenue East, Suite 700, Toronto, Ontario M4P 2Y3, Canada
(a division of Pearson Penguin Canada Inc.)
Penguin Books Ltd., 80 Strand, London WC2R 0RL, England
Penguin Group Ireland, 25 St. Stephen's Green, Dublin 2, Ireland (a division of Penguin Books Ltd.)
Penguin Group (Australia), 250 Camberwell Road, Camberwell, Victoria 3124, Australia
(a division of Pearson Australia Group Pty. Ltd.)
Penguin Books India Pvt. Ltd., 11 Community Centre, Panchsheel Park, New Delhi—110 017, India
Penguin Group (NZ), 67 Apollo Drive, Rosedale, North Shore 0632, New Zealand
(a division of Pearson New Zealand Ltd.)
Penguin Books (South Africa) (Pty.) Ltd., 24 Sturdee Avenue, Rosebank, Johannesburg 2196,
South Africa

Penguin Books Ltd., Registered Offices: 80 Strand, London WC2R 0RL, England

This book is an original publication of The Berkley Publishing Group.

Copyright © 2007 by Erin McCarthy.
Interior text design by Kristin del Rosario.

PRINTING HISTORY
Berkley Jam trade paperback edition / October 2007

Library of Congress Cataloging-in-Publication Data

Lynn, Erin.
   Demon envy / Erin Lynn. — Berkley JAM trade paperback ed.
      p.   cm.
   Summary: Levi, a water demon who seems very much like a teenage boy, emerges from a portal in sixteen-year-old Kenzie's bathroom one morning, and while his presence in her life is exasperating at times, he seems to help her fit in with her high-school peers.

   ISBN 978-0-425-21737-5 (Berkley JAM trade pbk.)
   [1. Demonology—Fiction.   2. High schools—Fiction.   3. School—Fiction.   4. Family life—Ohio—Fiction.   5. Ohio—Fiction.]   I. Title.

PZ7.L993De   2007
[Fic]—dc22   2007021055

PRINTED IN THE UNITED STATES OF AMERICA

10   9   8   7   6   5   4   3   2   1

Chapter One

Have you ever had such a horrible day that you wondered why your mother didn't just eat you at birth like a gerbil does and spare you the hassle?

We've all had days like that. I've had a *lot* of them—way more than my fair share if I want to be whiny about it (which I don't because I try really hard not to be a whiner), but none can compare to the day I accidentally opened a demon portal with my zit cream.

Oh, yeah. I did. Would this happen to anyone else? Probably not. But for me, Kenzie Sutcliffe, it is totally typical. If there is mud to step in, ketchup to squirt on my shirt, or a volleyball to be hit on the head with, I will manage it. What can I say? It's a gift.

October twentieth started out normal enough: The annoying

alarm went off way too early; mother made squawking sounds like a cracked-out parrot—*It's late, really late, you'll miss the bus!*; and brother turned my bedroom light on for spite, searing my sleep-deprived eyeballs with fluorescent lighting at six A.M. Major wardrobe disaster occurred when I discovered I hadn't turned on the dryer the night before and all my jeans were still cold and wet. Given that no one had done laundry in two weeks because Mom was working on a huge court case, I had finally taken matters into my own hands and stuffed eighty-seven pairs of jeans in the washer—literally every piece of denim I owned. Then somehow had forgotten to turn on the dryer after the transfer of pants from the washer. I remembered to empty the lint trap and add the Snuggle dryer sheet, but forgot to push the pesky little ON button.

Picture me in the kitchen, in frog pajama pants, staring into the dryer as if my retinas could evaporate all dampness: "Brandon! You were supposed to put the clothes in the dryer and turn it on!" It made me feel better to blame someone else even though it was a total out and out lie.

Fourteen-year-old brother, milk dribbling out of his mouth: "Bite me."

Okay, that was fair. Not bothering to pursue a good-natured round of verbal sparring with my brother, which wouldn't dry the jeans anyway, I ran back upstairs, mentally racing through my closet. Brown cords? Too earthy. Skirt? Too bohemian. Black pants? Too school band concert.

The thing is, I like jeans, and only jeans. Wearing anything else makes me feel like a photo layout in a teen magazine. Toss me a football, give me some shiny gloss and a fan blowing my hair here and there, and I could be the Fall Collection. The only reason I had the brown cords and the boho skirt and the band-concert pants was because my mother thought black hoodies were a crime against fashion humanity, and she held out a futile hope that by gifting me with cute coordinates, I would morph into Homecoming Queen destined for an Ivy League pre-law program. Much like herself.

It wasn't going to happen.

She would have to pass the tiara torch to my little sister, because I was purely Fringe. Not those dangly weird strips on the country-western shirts you see in seventies bar movies, but fringe, as in clinging to the edges of junior-class social acceptance. That was me. Never totally out but never totally in either. Just as likely to be included with an enthusiastic invite as totally forgotten when it comes time to pass the word on about a major party. I never knew which one I was getting, and it was frustrating.

But with so many of those offered friendships as fake as the glossy teen catazines, I was constantly waging a war with myself. Who wanted to hang with a bunch of hollaback girls? Or worse—be one. On the other hand, it sucked to spend Friday night at home watching *Rent* for the nineteenth time with my best friend Isabella. Principles vs. Popularity, the age-old question.

With this to debate while I showered, I went into my bathroom and discovered that a giant crater had surfaced on my chin overnight, a red-rimmed, oozing volcanic zit, ready to blow at any minute.

"Aah!" I shuddered involuntarily and reached for my morning acne lotion, the stuff that's slimy and bleaches the color out of my aqua blue hand towels. Occasionally I wonder if it's good to put something on my face that can strip color out of cotton—hello, Michael Jackson—but I need all the ammo I can get in the war on bad skin.

Here's where it got weird. I cranked up my CD player so I'd be able to hear it in the shower. Then, open bottle of lotion in my hand, I leaned over to turn on the water, wanting the temp to warm up while I was busy taking on pimple from hell in round one of Kenzie vs. Body Bacteria. I never even got as far as the faucet. In a move that is classic Kenzie—questioning the usefulness of all the hours and thousands of dollars spent on dance lessons if I couldn't even manage to walk without incident—I tripped on the bottom of my huge pajama pants and slammed into the wall, dropping the lotion into the tub. It bounced, I winced in pain, and fifty bucks' worth of prescription acne meds poured out of the bottle and down the drain.

I grabbed at it, but two-thirds was already gone. If the pipes were having problems with pimples, they'd be in luck; otherwise, it was a total waste. "Shoot!"

Saving what was left by tipping the bottle right side up, I

also grabbed a big glop that was still clinging to the rim of the drain and tried to dribble it back into the opened cap. Okay, I admit, that was kind of a gross thing to do, but the tub was clean and I was desperate. There was no way my mom would replace lotion that cost such major money just two weeks after I'd gotten it—can't you just smell the lecture?—and life with increased break outs was too horrific to contemplate.

Slapping what I couldn't force back into the bottle onto my crater-covered chin, I turned around to grope for a towel. Unfortunately they were all crumpled up, damp and dirty, on the floor where I had left them the night before, so I settled for swiping some toilet paper and trying to get the sticky slime off me.

My fingers were starting to burn and itch, which struck me as a bad sign. Like an allergic reaction waiting to happen. Like swelled sausage fingers or a nasty rash spreading out in ninety directions. And knowing my mother, that would not be a good enough reason to stay home from school. She'd make me go anyway, and by tomorrow my nickname would be Contagious Kenzie or Rash Girl. Notoriety for a dermatological emergency wasn't what I was going for, even if I had no interest whatsoever in making a play for homecoming queen.

Amber Janson already had that locked up anyway, even if we were only about a minute into our junior year. Barring a major scandal involving loss of her credit card privileges, announcement of a secret drug problem, or a sudden excessive weight gain, there were no challengers to Amber's dominance of the pack. Do I sound jealous? Yeah, guess what—it's because I was. Come on, you would be too. Honesty is a virtue, and I truly, honestly, loathed Amber. I'm not sure I had a good reason, exactly, since she'd never done anything to me directly. It was just that her life was like Bubblicious gum—pink and bouncy and full of sugar—and mine was a gumball—hard and totally lacking in flavor.

Wiping the lotion off my fingers wasn't working at all, and my skin was looking really red and annoyed. I was beginning to picture myself starring in a future Stephen King novel (*she was consumed by a giant rash!*), so I reached behind me to turn the shower on so I could rinse. Only my hand hit something hard, something that shouldn't have been there, something that was not shower wall, not faucet, not empty air like it should have been. And when I whipped my head around to check out what I'd made contact with, there was a guy sitting in my bathtub. Knees up to his chest, he blinked chocolate brown eyes at me.

There was a guy in my tub. *A guy.* In the tub.

You know what I did, right? I screamed bloody murder like any sane sixteen-year-old girl would do when a guy just randomly pops into her shower with zero warning. My mother didn't raise no fool.

She raised a chicken.

Or at least I tried to scream. Before I got halfway through one "Aaahhh," he cut me off by slapping his hand right over my mouth. I did *not* know he was going to do that. There was no time to react, no time to catch a breath, no time to jerk back, close my mouth or anything, before my face was suddenly covered with guy fingers from chin to nostrils. Not a good feeling. They were smothering and strong and they smelled like . . . guy. Like salted soft pretzel and skin. Totally disgusting.

I managed to yank my head back and opened my mouth to let loose with another yell when he did it again, this time actually squeezing my lips together.

"Dude, chill out with the screaming. It's obnoxious. And just who are you?" he asked, shock crossing his face as he checked me out, brown eyes flicking up and down.

Okay, I admit, I don't look all that hot before my shower—who does?—but he didn't need to look so appalled. And I could have already been showered and blow-dried, dragging on sweatpants and sliding on some lip color, if he hadn't just mysteriously appeared out of nowhere.

But of course he wasn't real. I had hit my head on the faucet and was unconscious and he was just the manifestation of my insecurities. It was the only explanation for why a brown-eyed geek was in my tub. He wasn't good-looking at all. Too skinny, ears sticking out a little, hair that needed a serious attempt at style, and a voice that sounded like Darth Vader, but two octaves higher. Total loser, and that was why this was a dream, an unconscious vision, because he was nothing to blog about, and yet *he* was dismissing *me* as unattractive.

How rude.

It had to be my subconscious telling me absolutely not to make a fool out of myself and ask Adam Birmingham to home-coming like I had been considering all week. (Not that I really would, but I was considering, which was me fooling myself un-til some other chick asked him first and I could then blame the ruination of my romantic dreams on her aggressiveness.)

Apparently my subconscious didn't know me all that well if it actually thought I would ever have the guts to approach Adam, and my subconscious was also sadly mistaken if it thought that by flashing a guy like this in front of me I would actually embrace realism—as in, *this* was the kind of guy I should be interested in, not Adam—it had another think coming. I preferred delusions to dorks. Sorry subconscious.

Trying not to make any sudden moves before I could deci-pher any further hidden meanings in this hallucination, I said, "Who am I? I'm Kenzie. Who are you? A manifestation of my fears? No, that would mean a serial killer with fuzzy hair would be in my tub, because tortured death and a bad hair day are truly my greatest fears. So maybe you're more like my impulse con-trol?"

Either way, I found it completely weird that anything gener-ated from my brain matter would use the word "dude." I have a personal vendetta against the overuse of it, but then again, maybe that meant something. It was symbolism for . . . something. Could be. I had no clue. Hey, we'd just started the psychology unit in social science. I hadn't gotten to visions and their relevance yet.

"Uh, actually, I'm a demon." He sat back against the shower wall and stretched his arms out, like he was testing them. When he unwound like that, he was broader than I expected, but he still looked like a high school Yu-Gi-Oh! champion. Not demonic at all, just dorky.

A demon. Wow, who knew my mind was so deep and dark? Maybe it was all the black hoodies and burgundy hair dye. But I wasn't following my subconscious on this one. I sat back on my heels. "I think I must have inhaled chemicals from the lotion. And what's the point of hallucinating if I can't figure out what it means?"

"Whoa, get a grip," he said. "No one here is hallucinating. I'm really a demon."

"No, you're not."

"Yes, I am."

"No, you're not. You're not even real."

He reached out and pinched my forearm. Hard.

"Ow! That hurt, loser." My arm had a nice red spot on it, above the mottled, rash-y fingers and wrist. Great. Add a bruise to my other deformities.

"That's because I'm real."

I was starting to wonder if he could actually be real.

"You're real? Not my subconscious trying to tell me something?" I was having a little trouble with this one even as the evidence moved around in front of me. I was totally lacking in luck or athletic ability, but not usually prone to encounters with otherworldly creatures.

"What would a guy in your shower be trying to tell you? That you missed a spot?"

"Okay, you're disgusting." It occurred to me that if I had been a little faster getting out of bed, I would have actually been *in* the shower when he appeared. That was a fate too horrible to contemplate.

"Look, I'm really a demon, okay? I've been locked in a prison portal for the last six months. You just freed me, so I owe you a thank-you." He stuck his hand out. "I'm Levi."

His name was definitely less dorky than he was. And I was getting used to his voice. It was slow and drawn out, nothing like the guys in suburban Ohio, where I'm stuck—I mean—live.

Not sure what else to do, I shook his hand. Yep. He felt pretty darn real. "I'm Kenzie. Why is there a demon portal in my shower?" And God, had he been hanging around in my drain for who knows how long? Listening to me sing in the shower? Had he been able to see anything? This could test the quality of my parents' mental-health insurance, because I would need counseling if he'd been watching me shower. "You need to leave. Now. You can go back the way you came, right?" I could shove him if I needed to. Pave the way for him with scrubbing bubbles.

"Didn't you hear me? I just escaped from a prison portal." He shook his head. "No chance I'm going back that way."

"Well, you have to go some way, obviously. And I'd love to hang around and chat about it, but I have to catch the bus." Mom wasn't going to take a demon appearing in my shower as a good excuse for having to drive me to school. The supernatural held no sway when she was due in court for a trial. And we won't mention the fact that I still had to take the bus in the first place because I had failed my driver's test. Twice.

A loud knock pounded on my bathroom door.

I jumped and Levi was suddenly standing in front of me, bouncing on the balls of his feet, fists up in a defensive, ready posture. "Stay behind me," he said.

Okay, now that was kind of hot. I'd like to think I could kick butt on my own, but it was nice to have a guy willing to do it for me. And he had moved fast. Freaky fast. He'd be a star on the soccer team, that's for sure.

"Kenzie!"

"It's just my five-year-old sister," I whispered. Levi relaxed his fists while I called, "What, Zoe?"

"Ka-en-za-ie! Mom says you're late."

Zoe had a way of drawing my name out into four syllables.

I was about to answer when she opened the bathroom door and strolled in. Zoe is adorable, with true blond hair (mine is that disgusting pseudo dirty-blond that just likes to pretend it's blond, so I dyed it dark brown with red highlights) and big blue eyes. She has the vocabulary of an eight-year-old, reads chapter books, and can rock a pair of black knee-high boots better than

11

I can. When I look at Zoe, I think that my parents experimented with Brandon and me, then finally got the DNA mix right with the third try. Her future was filled with a tiara.

"Who are you?" she asked Levi with a curious stare.

"You're supposed to knock before you come in," I said, going on the defensive as I stood up and moved around Levi to block him from view.

"I did. I knocked. Then I came in," she said with really annoying logic. Zoe is adorable, but she also has her fair share of brattiness. She's kind of like a puppy. Sweet to look at, fun to play with sometimes, but I don't think my parents really understood what they were getting into when they brought her into the house. She has the potential to be seriously destructive.

Perfect example—she looked us both over and said, "I don't think you're supposed to have a boy in your bathroom when you're wearing pajamas."

Yikes.

I pushed the button on the doorknob to lock the door and turned the shower water on so no one hanging around in the hall—like my brother, who was always seeking a way to blackmail me for cash—would hear the conversation.

"Okay, listen, I'll give you five bucks if you don't say anything to Mom."

She tightened her ponytail as she mulled it over. "Who is he?"

"This is Levi," I said.

"I'm Kenzie's boyfriend."

"Shut up!" I turned in horror. "That is *not* true, Zoe." As if. Please.

But she just nodded. "Okay, I won't say anything."

"Thanks." I gave a sigh of relief. "And he's leaving anyway. We just have to wait until Mom goes to work." Which would be *after* the bus came, a serious complication.

"Kenzie!" my mom yelled up the stairs. "What is taking you so long? The bus will be here in three minutes." I could hear her starting up the steps.

I panicked. "Ah!" I flipped up the toilet seat lid. "Zoe, you're sick, got it?"

My mom knocked on the door. "Kenzie, let's go! And where did Zoe disappear to?"

"She's in here, Mom. She's sick. She's barfing."

"Sick?" Annoyance changed to concern. "Zoe?"

Zoe leaned over and made first-class throw-up sounds, with lots of retching and choking.

Mom rattled the knob. "Unlock the door so I can come in."

"I can't, I'm in the shower." I leaned backward into the shower and stuck my head under the spray so my hair would be wet. It was cold and I shivered, but I stuck it out until I was adequately soaked. I turned off the water, threw a towel around myself, hoping my mom wouldn't notice I was still in my pajamas, and motioned for Levi to get in the shower. He did, pulling the curtain all the way across and giving Zoe a wink before he disappeared.

She giggled, then covered the laugh with a puke sound that would have shot her eyeballs out of her head if it were real.

"Oh, Zoe, honey."

My mom sounded really worried, so I took a washcloth, slapped water all over Zoe's face and hairline so she'd look sweaty, shoved the cloth in her hands, and flushed the toilet. I opened the door, heart pounding. Somehow I didn't think Mom was going to believe any "demon just popped into my tub without warning" explanation.

"I don't know what happened," I said. "She just came in here and started spewing."

Mom brushed past me and squatted down in her heels and chocolate suit. "Baby, are you feeling better?" She pushed back Zoe's hair and stuck her lips to my sister's forehead. "You're clammy."

Zoe gave a little moan and blinked pitiful eyes. The kid was so good, it was a little scary.

"I'm due at the courthouse in twenty minutes for opening remarks. Geez." Mom patted her hip pocket, looking for her cell phone. "This always happens when your father is traveling. He steps on a plane and someone throws up." She kissed the top of Zoe's head. "It's okay, baby. Let's get you into bed and I'll call Grandma. She should be able to get here in forty-five minutes and I'll just be a little late."

"I can stay home with her," I volunteered, seeing an opportunity and running with it. "Today is the end-of-the-quarter movie day. We're not doing anything important."

Okay, that was a total lie. I had an American history quiz and a book report I was supposed to present to my Lit class. But I also had a demon in my bathroom, and that outweighed Harpers Ferry facts and my summary of *Moby-Dick*. April Tyrell had been assigned the same book anyway, and once she said "lunatic goes after big whale," what else was left to say?

My mom had that tormented parental guilt look. Did she sacrifice my education and the possibility of an Ivy League college acceptance letter, or did she make it to her very important murder trial on time? She chose not to tick off the judge and give herself the best chance to convict the creep. Which was the right choice, because I had no intention whatsoever of applying to any school that had a political leader—any political leader—as an alumnus. I was going to attend drama school, but that was something of a secret at the moment.

"Okay. But keep her in the same room as you and don't let her watch too much TV. And call me if she doesn't stop throwing up."

"Got it."

Mom lifted Zoe and carried her down the stairs to set her up in the family room, which was sick kid central when someone stayed home. Zoe would get blankets, a pillow, a bucket, the remote control, and some ginger ale. With that kind of day of leisure ahead of her, she should be paying *me* five bucks, not the other way around. Then again, she was in kindergarten. Her most strenuous school activities were finger painting with shaving cream and accepting gifts of cookies from her many five-year-old male admirers. Zoe got more action with guys than I did, any day of the week.

"Let me get dressed. I'll be down in a second," I said and shut the door, locking it.

"Are you gone?" I whispered to the black shower curtain, hoping the whole thing had been a weird wrinkle in time and now my normal boring life had been restored. I would never wish for excitement again—Satan might pop up on my PC screen next.

The shower curtain yanked back. My demon looked annoyed. "Yes, I'm still here. And I have wet feet." Levi lifted up his gym shoe to prove his point. It did look a little shiny.

"Do demons melt in water?" I tried not to sound too hopeful.

"No. Water is my element."

"Then quit complaining! We almost got busted."

"I think that would be more of a problem for you than it would be for me."

Exactly. I was worried about me, not him. Guy-in-my-tub had Grounded For Life written all over it. "As soon as my mom leaves, you can go out the back door."

He stepped out of the tub and carelessly pulled up his jeans a little. He was taller than I had realized and I was suddenly aware that I was still in my pajamas with zit cream on my chin. I was starting to feel a little irritated. I had enough reasons to stress—bad skin, play tryouts on Saturday, homecoming inching closer and closer with no date, that really irritating issue of no driver's license—I didn't have time for this. And if he thought for one minute I was going anywhere in public with him, he was so wrong. No way. I couldn't risk anyone getting the wrong idea. If word got around I was dating a less-than-hot demon, my life would be ruined, absolutely over. I'd have to dye my hair (back to dirty blond, no thanks) and change schools.

"Why did you tell Zoe you're my boyfriend? What if she says something to my mom?"

"What was I supposed to do, tell the kid I'm a demon? She'd have run out of here screaming and had nightmares for the rest of her life. I don't scare little kids, man." He looked offended by the very thought.

"You didn't have any problems telling me you were a demon."

"And you didn't get scared, did you? You looked like you could handle the truth, except for a minute there where you went on that stupid psychobabble trip and thought I was like your conscience or something. But aside from that, you handled it alright. Besides, you saw me pop out of the portal. You saw for yourself I wasn't human."

"You're not human?" That, more than anything else, was the freakiest thing I had ever heard.

"Try to keep up with me," he said very slowly, like I was a candidate for the short bus. "De-mon. Demon. Me demon, you teenage girl."

Irritated, I rolled my eyes. He might not have been human, but he had enough testosterone to make him a complete and total jerk.

"Way to be annoying."

He smiled. "But I'm cute."

"Not." I put my hand on the doorknob. "Do not leave this bathroom until I say it's okay."

"Do I get five bucks if I listen to you?"

"No. You don't get your demon butt kicked by me."

He had picked up my T-shirt and was studying it, not looking the least bit intimidated. "Wow, okay, since I'm now terrified."

"Give me that!" I pulled the shirt out of his hands. "Don't touch anything."

I slipped out the door, careful to only open it a crack, and closed it behind me. Maybe with a little luck by the time I got back he would have vaporized.

But we all know the indisputable truth—I never have any luck.

Chapter Two

When I opened the bathroom door ten minutes later, after shooing my mother out the door and checking on Zoe, I fought the urge to smack my demon. Violence with an escaped underworld convict probably wasn't a very swift idea, so I restrained myself.

Yet I couldn't help but glare at him. "What are you doing? God!"

Levi was standing in front of my bathroom mirror, brushing his teeth. With my purple toothbrush. He spit out a frothy mouthful. "Brushing my teeth. Six months in lockup is a long time to go without being able to brush, man. I was really worried about gingivitis."

"You haven't brushed your teeth in six months?" Eew.

"I haven't been able to take a shower either."

Double eew.

"I would have taken one but you don't have any fresh towels in your bathroom. Could you go grab me one?"

Was he serious? Did I have demon servant written on my sleep shirt?

"I haven't even had a shower yet!"

"You'd better use another bathroom then," he said, wiping his demon mouth on my blue towel.

"Excuse me?" I put my hand on my hip, not feeling much like a Happy Hostess. "This is my house, and my bathroom. You can wait until I'm done."

"Okay, but I'm not sure why I wound up here in the first place. And while I think I closed the portal behind me, there's always the possibility that someone else might come through."

That rolled around in my brain for a minute while he rummaged through my drawers and found some dental floss. Was he saying . . . "Are you saying another demon could come into my shower?"

"At any time, without any warning, yep." Levi twisted a strand of floss around his fingers and leaned toward the mirror.

"Ohmygawd." I think I whimpered. "No . . . Then that means I can't use my bathroom at all. Ever." The potential horrors were endless if a random demon showed up while I was doing literally anything I would normally do in my bathroom.

I mean, what if I was in . . . or then I was on . . . I shuddered. It was so stomach-acid churning and potentially disgusting I couldn't even finish my thoughts.

"Probably not a good idea." He flashed his teeth to the mirror. "Much better. Now how about that towel, Kenzie?"

A happy, hopeful thought came to me: "If I give you a towel and let you shower, will you leave and take your demon portal with you?" It would really just be better all around if the whole demon thing slipped quietly away. I could barely handle my life without creatures from hell. There was no way I could Buffy my way through a bunch of Satan sidekicks hanging out in my bathroom.

"I can't take it with me. A portal is a portal. Did you do something to open it? Something different from what you normally do in the morning? There had to be a reason I popped through." He tossed his used floss in the wastebasket and studied me curiously.

"I, uh, dropped my lotion down the drain."

"Lotion? That shouldn't have been powerful enough to have any effect. Huh. What kind of lotion? Was it herbal or something? You know a lot of that herbology has its origins in witchcraft. In the sixteenth century—"

And I cared because . . . ? I cut him off before he went into the History of the World According to Dorked-Out Demons. "It was a prescriptive topical lotion."

His eyebrows shot up. "Where is it?"

Biting my lip, I handed him the bottle, almost empty and slightly sticky.

Levi read the bottle, his lips moving silently. Then he nodded. "Ah. Hydrochloric acid. That stuff is potent in the otherworld. So what do you use this lotion for?"

"My skin."

It took him a second, then he grinned. "It's zit cream, isn't it? And despite having like ninety chemicals in it, it doesn't even work." His finger tapped my chin. "You've got a shiner right now."

"Ah!" I gasped, yanked the bottle out of his hands, and slapped it down on the counter. "The towels are in the linen closet in the hall. You can get one yourself. Then while you're washing your slimy demon body, you can figure out how to get yourself back to where you came from, because you can't stay here. I mean it. I will *scream* if you're not gone by the time my mom gets home."

"Geez, take a pill, Kenzie. No need to go all PMS on me."

Oh, really? I gritted my teeth. "Is it possible to murder a demon? Because I *totally* don't like you."

"Well, I *am* a demon. It's not like you're supposed to want to rub my belly or anything."

My stomach threatened to make like Zoe and retch at that image. "Thanks for making me want to yak."

"I've had a long time to perfect it." He smiled.

I turned around and slammed the bathroom door shut behind

me, enjoying the sharp sound it made. He started to sing, turning my CD player up.

My demon could cut glass with that off-key warbling.

And he didn't sound like he was in any hurry to leave.

Which could be a serious problem.

With Levi taking over my ultra-cool bathroom, with its black (*Yes, Mom, black. Yes, I really do want black. No, I am not preoccupied with death.*) and aqua-blue color scheme, I was forced to go down the hall to Brandon and Zoe's bathroom. I was tempted to go into my mom and dad's master bath and luxuriate in a four-head shower experience, but my mother had a mop that she kept in the closet and used after each shower to suck every last inch of water off the doors, the tile, and the floor to keep it clean. I didn't have time for that kind of obsessive-compulsive, anal-retentive behavior. I had a demon to evict from the premises.

So I stepped into flip-flops to protect my feet from Brandon-generated fungus and went down to the hall bathroom. I supposed I should have felt guilty that my fourteen-year-old, nearly six-foot-tall brother had to share a bathroom with his five-year-old sister. But I didn't. Wasn't feeling it at all. Because if Brandon wasn't sharing with Zoe, I would be, and she'd have her little paws in my makeup on a daily basis. I could dredge up some occasional sympathy for Brandon, but sisterly affection didn't extend to coughing up my bathroom digs. Besides, I think Mom didn't want Zoe in my bathroom because she didn't want to have to explain to her what tampons were. Worked for me.

Once I waded through the maze of cast-off pajamas and abandoned towels on the floor, I managed a quick shower, with a whole crowd of naked Barbies and Disney princesses. Hopefully they were all Zoe's, or my brother was a freak. I realized I'd forgotten my razor, but I was going to have to pretend my legs and armpits weren't hairy just for one day. Since it was October, I figured I'd just cover everything up and stress about it later.

When I got downstairs, after doing a lame blow-dry job, hair frizzy at the ends, I found Levi and Zoe all cozy in the family room playing Go Fish. Zoe was sipping a Coke and looking at Levi like he was Prince Charming to her Snow White.

"She's not supposed to have Coke," I said, annoyed for so many reasons I couldn't pick the one that was heading the list at the moment.

"Why not?" he asked as Zoe sucked on the straw harder, clearly afraid I was going to yank it away from her.

"Caffeine is bad for kids. She can't drink it until she's ten."

"Well, that's not fair."

"Yes, it is."

"No, it's not. When you were five, you were the oldest child and there was no one drinking Coke in front of you. Zoe has to watch you and your brother drink it right in front of her. It's inhumane, unfair."

"Yeah." Zoe stopped sucking and gave me an indignant look, followed by a massive carbonation-created burp.

"Did we ask you?" I said.

"I'm just saying . . ." He held his hand out like he was being wronged right along with Zoe.

"How do you get your wings so shiny?" Zoe said, patting the air next to Levi.

"What?" I asked.

Levi's head whipped around and he stared at Zoe. "You can see my wings?"

"Your wings?" I asked. "You have *wings*?"

Levi shot me an annoyed look. "One more time, Kenzie. I'm a demon. Yes, I have wings."

"I don't see any wings."

"I do," Zoe said. "And they have blue and green scales."

Scales? Hello. "Ohmygawd!" Scooting around him, I reached for Zoe. "Don't touch my sister, you . . . you . . . creature."

"Oh, relax. I'm not going to hurt you. I'm a really nice guy as far as demons go. That's why I was in prison, you know."

I was trying to yank Zoe up by the waist, but she had obviously gained ten pounds when I wasn't looking. The kid was heavy and all I managed to do was arch her back and make her legs jerk. "In my experience . . ." I heaved and tugged. "Zoe, put your arms around me. People go to prison because they're not nice. You know, like criminals."

Zoe fought me instead, pushing her hands in my face, and

I half fell over her on the couch, my knee clipping the coffee table. Brat. And here I was busting my behind to save her.

Levi put his hand on the back of my black T-shirt and hauled me to a standing position. "Not demons. I was put in prison because I had very minimal demonic activity."

"What does that mean?" I was breathing hard, and I tucked back my hair, tugging my shirt down over my bare stomach. "You haven't eaten any children lately?"

"I'm so misunderstood." Levi put his feet on the coffee table. "I see I'm going to have to explain a thing or two to you."

"I can hardly wait." And since he wasn't leaving, and I wasn't leaving without Zoe, who wasn't leaving without a fight, it looked like we were all staying. Defeated, I collapsed onto the butter-yellow chair opposite the couch.

"Have you ever heard of the seven deadly sins?"

"No."

"The seven deadly sins are responsible for all vice in humans. They rank from least awful to worst, and each one leads you deeper into sin. It is a demon's job to encourage humans to sin by providing you with temptations."

Now I really didn't like him. "What are the seven deadly sins?" And which one was he trying to tempt me to do? I shivered, rubbing my hands over my arms. Was something touching me?

"Lust, gluttony, greed, sloth, wrath, envy, and pride."

Well, that did seem to sum it all up. All the basic Bad Things. "What's sloth?"

"Laziness."

I definitely knew a few people who were fond of that sin, starting with half of my high school.

"What's lust?" Zoe asked.

"Um . . ." I couldn't come up with an appropriate definition for a five-year-old to hear, but I knew I felt a sixteen-year-old version of it when I looked at Adam Birmingham.

"It's an obsessive desire for another person," Levi told her.

Yep. That's exactly what I felt when Adam strolled into anatomy and physiology every day.

"What's obsessive mean?"

"It means you always want to be with that person, every minute."

"Oh." Zoe and I thought that one through.

I couldn't vouch for what was going through her still-emerging mind, but I was thinking about Adam and how utterly perfect we could be for each other if he would just lift his testosterone-soaked skull and actually look at me for once. Since we were lab partners we talked almost every day, but he was very skilled at discussing scientific method without actually ever turning toward me. He always slouched in his chair, studying his papers, long legs sticking out from under the front of our lab table, and he had gorgeous black hair, a nice voice, and a modicum of intelligence. A normal, nice, good-looking guy, who very possibly was even In My League, except for the fact that he was an uberathlete. In the fall he played soccer *and* used his golden foot as a placekicker for the football team. The administration was so enamored of his ability to arch that ball though the posts, they exempted him from the majority of football practices so he could juggle both sports. In the winter he swam, and spring was for baseball.

Okay, so who was I kidding? I couldn't even roller blade or play laser tag. I was theatrical, as my father liked to say. Music and acting. But who said the athlete and the artist couldn't find common ground over the dissection of a fetal pig?

Hope lived on.

Zoe touched the tip of her tongue to her nose, then commented, "Then I guess Chase has lust for me. He always wants to sit next to me at circle time."

Yikes. I glared at Levi. "If she gets kicked out of kindergarten, I'm holding you responsible." Then my eyes went wide and I grabbed my chest. "Ohmygawd! You did that on purpose. That was a demon trick. . . . You're trying to get us in trouble."

"No. I'm trying to explain. I belong to the demon sect of Envy. I'm supposed to encourage envy, jealousy, the desire for material possessions in humans. But I was slacking, only doing the bare minimum because I wanted out. I started thinking there was more to life than stirring up trouble for humans, you know what I'm saying? So I got tossed in prison. It was a raw deal."

At least he wasn't the demon of lust. I did not want to be influenced into liking someone gross against my will. Like him. "So you're a demon trying to reform your demonic ways?" Yeah, that sounded legit. Not.

He smiled and batted his eyelashes. "Yes. Don't you feel my pain and suffering? Don't you want to help me?"

"Not really." But rarely did anyone ever care what I wanted. (Okay, that sounded whiny, didn't it? So pretend I didn't say that. Gone. I did not want to be a whiner, honestly.)

"I'll help you," Zoe said, petting the air next to him again. It occurred to me that she was petting the wing I couldn't see, which was a serious freak-out.

"Thanks, shortie." He gave me a smug look. "*She* likes me."

"She also eats dog food if you ask her to." I touched the zit on my chin and tried to think. Unbelievable or not, I had a demon on my couch, and by helping him, I would also be helping myself. By getting him out of my house. "So, if I help you, will you go away? And help you do what, exactly?"

"Escape my servitude permanently."

Hello, details, please. I wasn't agreeing to anything vague. "By"—I moved my hand to encourage more info—"doing what, exactly?"

"I'm not really sure, specifically. I don't think anyone has ever permanently escaped, or at least not so we heard about it. But I figure if I can elude my captors and I don't starve, I'll have a good shot at being my own demon."

"You mean you'll always be a demon? You won't become a real guy?" What a rip-off.

"What am I, Pinocchio? I'm a real boy," he mocked, then rolled his eyes. "No, I won't be human. But I just want to be left alone." He gave me a pleading look. "Please, Kenzie, I'm so tired of this gig. You don't know what it's like, the pressure to force people into vice. It's exhausting."

Okay, I felt sorry for him. I admit it. He looked so sincere, so sweet, so puppy-dog kind of cute. And how awful would it be to run around whipping up trouble for people? No one would like you, and it sounded lonely to me.

I leaned forward in compassion, unable to ignore that kind of plaintive need. I mean, how cruel could I be? He wanted to change, be one of the good guys for once, or at least be left alone, never having to force people to do nasty things again. It was like when Darth Vader, after a complete adulthood of evil deeds, couldn't bring himself to kill Luke, and struggled to turn away from the dark side. . . . What if Luke had gone all stubborn on him and abandoned Daddy Darth right then? Walked away? Vader never would have had the chance to take that gross helmet off, and the movie would have had a really sucky ending.

"What can I do to help?" I asked, feeling just terrible for him and his dilemma, not to mention so sorry that the whole thing was making me think in *Star Wars* metaphors.

He smiled. "I knew I could count on you. You're awesome, Kenzie. So, here's the plan . . ."

Stupid + gullible = Kenzie Sutcliffe.

He was so playing me.

Chapter Three

Levi's Plan to escape demonic indentured servitude, as recorded by Kenzie Sutcliffe, age sixteen, junior at West Shore High School, who can't figure out how she got sucked into being secretary for the rude guy with invisible wings:

1. Convince Kenzie's mother to let me (oops, I mean Levi. This secretarial crap is harder than I thought, because he is telling me in first person, but I'm recording in third person since we are both going to read this list, not just him, therefore *I* is not solely referring to him. But now that I've totally confused myself, I'd better start over) SO . . . (1) Convince Kenzie's mother to let Levi move in for a while.

"Hold it," I said, after typing that little bit of insanity into my PDA. "You're cracked if you think I'm going to let you move into my house." I was glad Zoe had ventured off to her room to play. I didn't need her stumping for Levi's Live-In campaign, because there was no way I was going to let him invade my life to that extent.

"You said you'd help me."

"I meant I could like buy you a burger for lunch, let you use my shower—which I've already done—and maybe send you on your way with ten bucks. I did not mean move in with me."

"I'm not talking about sharing your room, Kenzie. I just meant crashing on the couch for a few days."

Spots danced in front of my eyes at the thought of him setting foot in my bedroom. "No."

Levi was slouched on the couch, feet still on the coffee table, the laces on his gym shoes dirty and worn. His sweatshirt and jeans looked soft and faded, like they'd been around the block nine hundred times. I winced at the thought that they hadn't been washed in six months. If denial of bathing privileges was a form of psychological torture, I'd better toe the line. I couldn't imagine the impact not washing my hair daily would have on my mental health.

"Then how can I make sure the portal is closed?" he said.

"You're referring to this prison portal in my shower?" I was really trying to ignore that little fact.

"Yes. I need to be here until we're sure it's closed. Because only two kinds of demons could come through—prisoners or prison guards."

"Oh, geez. I'm getting a headache." I rubbed my temples. "But didn't you say that in the demon world prisoners are good demons?"

"Well . . . sometimes. Like in my case. But mostly, uh, no," Levi told the coffee table, not meeting my eyes at all.

"Wonderful. So psycho demons from Hell or the guards who imprison them could pop out of my drain at any time? Fabulous. Thanks for playing."

"Demons aren't really from Hell, you know. The dudes in Hell are the fallen angels who were cast out of Heaven."

"Wow, great. You're not from Hell, but you spend all your time convincing humans to sin. Got it. Now that *that's* all cleared up."

"You need to get a handle on that sarcasm. It's really the only thing about you that's totally unattractive."

"Unattractive?" I was totally offended. And didn't he know that my sarcasm was a defense mechanism because I was actually slightly (just mildly) insecure? Everyone in theater was. If he didn't know that, he should. "Look, if you don't like me, or any of my personality traits, you can leave. It will not break my heart."

"I leave, you'll have to deal with the situation all on your own if any demons appear in your shower."

Smack. He had me on that one.

"Number two," he said, holding up two fingers.

2. Register for school.

"What school? Why?" Maybe he was talking about cooking school or swimming school or private school for demons hanging out on Earth. You know, like a demon magnet school. St. Lucifer's Academy of Demonic Possession.

"Your school. West Shore High, right?"

I closed my eyes. No, no, no. I very carefully opened my eyes and spoke slowly, calmly. "Why do you need to go to my school? Why would anyone willingly register for school if they didn't have to?"

"I'm blending, going incognito, man. And if I'm going to make this escape thing work, I've got to make my way in the world, you know. Get a degree like everyone else. I have demon talents, sure, but they'll only take me so far."

Positive I didn't want to know what those talents might be, I tried to find a way out. "You should go to Westlake High. It's bigger, huge. No one will even notice you. My school is kind of small and you'll stick out as the new kid."

"But this is my address." He pointed to the carpet. "Your house. It will be fine. I'll be your cousin from out of town."

That made it all okay, then. Now I was supposed to be *related* to him.

3. Find alternative source of sustanence.

That didn't look right. "How do you spell that?"

"Spell what?"

"Sustenance," I said, really working my jaw around it. What a five-dollar word. My demon was articulate. And I was going to bomb on the SAT.

"S-u-s-t-e-n-a-n-c-e."

"Damn, I mixed up the *e* and the *a*."

"I don't mind. Move on."

"Why do you need an alternative sustenance? Alternative to what?"

"I feed off other people's envy. If I'm not making people envious or jealous, then I starve."

"Oh. Well, that totally sucks." And was disturbing, creepy, grotesque, frightening, mind-blowing . . .

"Tell me about it. If I want to give up inciting sin, I'll starve. So I have to find another way to sustain myself."

"How about pizza? That always sustains me for a while."

"Cute. But not even close."

"What about drinking human blood like vampires do? Disgusting, but not stirring up trouble like making people envious."

"Okay, how about I drink your blood and we'll test it?"

I grabbed my neck and recoiled. Levi started laughing.

"I'm kidding, Kenzie. Give me a break."

I threw a pillow at him, and my heart rate slowly returned to normal. "So this is it? Just three things on your list? That's not a To-Do List, that's just optimism."

"Number four—world domination. Number five—always be myself. Number six—get a haircut. Number seven—convince Kenzie to fall in love with me, get married, and buy a minivan." He rolled his eyes so far back it's a wonder he didn't lose them in his skull.

"Now who is being sarcastic?"

But I had to secretly admit, I thought he was just a tiny bit funny when he wasn't being annoying.

"My mom's going to kill me," I said when I went to answer the doorbell. "She is not going to like that I am ditching Zoe."

"It will be fine. We'll be back before she even gets home," Levi answered, running his hand through his shaggy hair. "There's just a couple of things I need to do."

Zoe was entranced by prancing ponies on the TV and didn't look worried that we were leaving her with my best friend, Isabella. I opened the door and Isabella sashayed in. Isabella doesn't walk—she sashays, prances, bounces, floats. She is a dancer and always has her feet slightly pointed out in first position. She weighs like three pounds, has legs that go up to my neck, and hair that knows what color it wants to be—ink black.

Absentminded sometimes, an awesome friend always, she is also extremely compassionate. I knew she would understand my plight, even if Levi had told me I couldn't reveal his demon origins to her. She would understand how awful it was to have a relative (what we were calling the demon) in my house, upsetting my schedule and preventing me from the comfort of wearing pajamas in my own home.

"So why weren't you in school today?" she asked, dumping her backpack on the tile floor of the kitchen and peeling off her pea coat.

"Zoe was sick this morning, but she is fine now, and I have to go pick up my homework and my cousin is here and he really needs to do something but I swear, I totally swear, Iz, that we'll be back in like an hour. You are so sweet to do this and I owe you seriously big-time massively for the rest of my life."

I could have saved the groveling. She was no longer listening but was smiling at Levi, her hands going into the back pockets of her very tight, very low-riding jeans.

"Hi."

"Hey, what's up," Levi said back as they locked eyes, checked each other out.

Flirt, flirt, smile, smile.

Yuck, yuck.

"This is my cousin, Levi. He's from . . . Ontario."

"Canada? Cool," Isabella said, still smiling. "I'm Isabella. How long are you staying?"

"It's kind of up in the air, but probably the rest of the school year."

What?!? What happened to a couple of days? Levi went over to the couch to say something to Zoe and Isabella turned to me, grabbing my arm. "He's staying for months?" she whispered.

"Yes. Isn't that awful? Iz, I don't think I'll be able to survive it." I thought I was actually having a panic attack just imagining it. Had I developed asthma overnight? Because I was suddenly having trouble breathing. Your junior year is supposed to be the definitive year, the year you lock in your grades and extracurricular activities, the year you look ahead to college while diving headlong into a seriously committed relationship with a member of the opposite sex, *not* the year you have a demon masquerading as your cousin, sharing your bathroom towels.

"Awful? He's adorable. If you don't want him here, send him to my house." She grinned.

"Adorable? Excuse me while I go puke."

"Put in a good word for me," she whispered, wrapping her arm through mine as Levi strolled back over to us. "You know, mention I don't have a boyfriend, how I like Canadian food . . . Hi." She smiled brightly at Levi.

"Canadian food?" I asked. "What the heck is considered Canadian food? French fries with vinegar?"

"Ahhahaha." Isabella gave a very phony laugh, then turned and glared at me.

"You sure you're okay staying with Zoe?" Levi asked her.

"Not a problem. I don't mind at all. I love children."

That was news. Isabella liked the ballet, classic rock, clothes, and chocolate. It was her life's ambition to leave Ohio for Chicago and the professional dance world as soon as she could. I had never once heard her profess a great love of children.

"Cool. Zoe's fine just watching TV until we get back. You probably shouldn't let her have any more Coke though."

Who was he, Zoe's dad?

Surrogate brother maybe. Zoe came hurtling over to Levi and wrapped her arms around his legs. "You're coming back, right?"

"Yep. Be good, shortie." He tossed her back and forth from leg to leg a few times, making her ponytail bounce. Then he let her go, giving her a teasing shove so that she stumbled forward, looking like my aunt Mary when she's had four glasses of wine. The similarity grew when Zoe took a facer into the couch.

"Hey, Iz, can I borrow your car?" I asked.

That diverted her attention from checking out Levi's butt in his jeans. "No way. You don't have a license, and you know my mom has the ability to materialize out of thin air whenever I'm doing something I shouldn't be. If she saw you driving my car, we'd both be toast."

"I have my temps." I'd had those for quite a freaking while, actually.

"Forget it."

I made a face. "I guess we'll have to walk then."

No one seemed to feel sorry for me.

"Bye," Levi said to Isabella with a friendly wave.

"Bye," she whispered back, her standard dreamy expression dreamier than usual.

When we walked out the front door, I grabbed him by the arm and said, "Don't touch her."

"What? Who, Zoe? Why not?" To his credit, he did actually look confused.

"Not Zoe. Isabella. Do not molest my friend."

"*Molest* your friend? What do I look like?"

"A demon!" I snapped.

He made that sound. That incredibly annoying guy sound that is like air and indignation leaving their mouth at the same time, like they're really saying "we know everything because we are male, and you, as a female, will never understand what I'm trying to tell you." Usually this happens in discussions about sports or relationships, and then you might as well just pack it up. They're done talking. It's at that point in talks with my mother that my father gets obsessed with channel surfing.

That rude guy sound brought out the militant feminist in me, the one who reared her head occasionally without warning when I felt the weight of male injustice. At the moment, I even had the hairy armpits to go along with my indignation, thanks to being forced out of my bathroom. "What?" I snarled.

Levi just shook his head. "Don't worry about your friend."

I was too worried about Isabella to appreciate the effort of him saying I shouldn't worry. "Wow, I'm so reassured."

"That hurts, Kenzie. That just hurts."

"Whatever. Where are we going? Do we really have to walk somewhere?" We were standing in the driveway and I was wishing I'd grabbed a coat. The wind was cutting through my hooded sweatshirt.

"School."

"We're really going to school?" I asked, following him as he started toward the street. "And I hate walking, by the way. I'm not really athletic."

"That shocks me completely and totally."

"My strengths are more intellectual in nature. Except for spelling. And I can sing."

"No kidding?"

"No, I'm not kidding." I surveyed our progress. We were now half a house down from mine. "The high school is all the way down Mills Road. It's going to take us half an hour to walk there."

"We'll live."

Was I getting a stitch in my side? I absently rubbed it over my sweatshirt. "Easy for the demon to say."

Levi bit his fingernail and didn't say anything.

"If I had known I was going to have to hike two miles up to school, I would have eaten a snack before we left."

He stayed silent.

"You know, it's not my fault I don't have my license. Both times were just screwed up. I got the same old lady and she had some kind of vendetta against me." I fumed just remembering the shock of seeing FAILED stamped on my application—twice. "She nitpicked me. Said I had slow reactions. But she totally set me up to fail by driving me through the ghetto. The ghetto. I'm serious. You couldn't even see the lines on the street there were so many potholes, so how could she know if I was a foot out of the turn lane or not? Not to mention that she jeopardized my personal safety the second time by insisting I turn onto a street that had a huge group of guys hanging around in front of what was probably a crack house. You would have gone sixty miles an hour too if you had seen the hand gesture one of them gave me."

It was actually kind of nice to have someone new to commiserate with. Isabella refused to hear any more about how my driving rights had been violated. Besides, the renewed indignation over being the only loser still taking the bus as a junior was keeping my mind off my sudden intense hunger as we walked. I need to eat every two hours without fail.

"I'm starving. I really should have grabbed a snack. I have a very high metabolism, you know. I burn calories like crazy. I know some girls hate me for that, but I can't help it. I'm naturally tall and thin, and truthfully, I'd love to be just a little shorter. Being five-nine doesn't do much good if you don't play basketball. It just makes it hard to find sandals."

Levi glanced over at me, but still didn't say anything. It occurred to me that he was ignoring me.

We trudged past two more houses.

"So, you know, it's probably a good thing I don't do any extensive physical activity. I'd waste away. I'd be like a walking skeleton. Of course . . ." I was starting to get out of breath, so I sucked in some air. "If I did sports maybe I wouldn't be such a klutz, you know? Dance was supposed to give me grace, but it failed miserably. I am flexible though."

Nothing. I was starting to feel offended as well as hungry and tired. What good was talking if he didn't talk back? "I think I have a cramp in my leg."

Levi sighed. "Kenzie, why don't you get on my back so you don't have to walk."

Hello. "Oh, that's okay, no thanks, I'm fine." Though that offer was kind of nice. Sweet. Thoughtful. "God, I'm hungry. My stomach is digesting its own lining."

Levi glanced back at me. "Do you hear that?" He stopped and tilted his head.

"No, what is it?" I looked around, wary. Maybe a prison guard had found Levi. As much as I'd like to help, I didn't want to be caught in the middle of that mess. But I had a hard time picturing me being able to outrun a demon warden. I'd probably lose a race to Zoe.

"It's the sound of silence when there are no teenage girls whining."

I gasped. "I'm not whining!"

"Yes, you are. Whine, whine, whine. Bitch, moan, cry."

Well. That seemed like an exaggeration. Sort of.

"And if anyone is starving here, it's me. At least you can eat. I can't."

Ah. The poor guy, I had completely forgotten he wasn't eating at all. That whole "trying to be good" thing must be really hard for him, and here I was going on and on about being a bottomless pit that eats constantly.

Okay, so I may be whiny (on rare occasions before I catch myself) and sarcastic (frequently), but I'm *always* compassionate.

"I'm sorry, Levi, I forgot. Isn't there anything we can do? You must feel sick."

"Actually, it makes me tired, and the hunger is kind of like a burning in my gut. It's getting worse."

Now that I looked at him, I realized he was pale and his forehead looked a little shiny, like he was sweating. "There must be something we can do."

He ran his hand across the leaves of a bushy hedge next to the sidewalk. "Just keep talking to distract me. . . . I don't know, just name someone you don't like."

It took me less than a microsecond to produce a name. "Amber? Why should I think about Amber?"

"Why don't you like Amber?"

"Because she's perfect. Her dad is the mayor, her mother is a surgeon, she's athletic *and* smart, and she never, ever gets acne.

She has a blue Mini Cooper that matches her eyes, as she tells everyone repeatedly. Nothing bad ever happens to her. She could probably wet her pants and somehow it would be considered cool." I clapped my mouth shut. That was a bit snarky. I didn't really care that much. Did I?

"Is she pretty?"

"If you like blondes." Which every guy does.

"Does she have a boyfriend?"

"Of course."

"What did she get for her last birthday?"

I gritted my teeth. This one had gotten under my zit-covered skin, I admit it. "Her parents took her to New York for the weekend and they saw *Wicked* on Broadway." Amber didn't even like the theater. She couldn't have cared less that she got to see a show that I would give my brother to see (okay, that's not a big sacrifice, I would actually like to give Brandon away, so switch to—I would give up my entire wardrobe to see *Wicked*).

"Were you jealous?"

"Yes." Insanely, putridly, pulse-pounding jealous.

I looked over at Levi, who had stopped walking. His eyes were closed, fists clenched. He sucked in a deep, shuddering breath, and sighed. Unclenching his hands, he opened his brown eyes. They were sharp, relieved, and he ran a thumb over his bottom lip, like he'd just taken a nice long drink.

Which maybe he had. Yikes.

As I stood there, stunned, his shoulders straightened, his

skin filled with color, and a cocky grin crossed his face. "Thanks," he said.

"Oh, oh, oh . . ." I took a step back, stomach tight. I knew that he had been starving, and without meaning to I had just taken the edge off of that hunger. That wasn't a bad thing in theory, but . . . "That was wrong. We shouldn't have done that, Levi."

"Oh, come on. What's a little jealousy between friends? I'll die if I don't eat."

But I felt a little sick and ashamed of myself for some weird reason. "Levi . . ."

He took my hand and pulled me next to him.

Freaked out on so many levels, I jerked back, ripping my hand from his. Which of course twisted my foot, and I promptly fell off the edge of the sidewalk, and wound up just about sitting on a bush.

While Levi hauled me out of the hedge, I said, "I *really* don't like walking."

"Next time you won't turn down my offer."

"What offer?"

"To ride on my back."

I eyed him. Was I really going to do this?

Apparently I was. I jumped on his back and suddenly we were moving NASCAR speed.

Chapter Four

My mother doesn't know this, because she would have a kitten, but I rode on a motorcycle once with the director of the last show I was in. I know, not exactly a dangerous or daring thing to confess, but nonetheless, parental knowledge of it would have landed me in some kind of motor vehicle safety course and a two-week grounding from anything even remotely fun. It was no big deal. We were just going to a cast party, and yes, loser me didn't have a ride—have I mentioned I have NO LICENSE? So Dave, who is fifty and gay (which is only relevant in that it exempts him from the seeming perversion of offering to take a sixteen-year-old girl on the back of his chopper), gave me a lift.

Moving at high speed on a bucket of bolts held up only by

the strength in Dave's skinny thighs was both terrifying and exhilarating. That wind zipping past me, and the feeling of being inside a fast-paced video game was seriously cool. Though scary.

That's what riding on Levi's back was like—the thrill of the speed countered with the total fear of seeing trees go by in a blink. The cool wind was stinging my eyes and making my nose run, and I clung to Levi like a baby monkey, afraid I'd be flung to the ground in a painful sprawl if I loosened my hold. The twenty-minute walk was sliced to about two mind-boggling minutes where I gripped his shoulders, stared straight ahead in wonder, and kept my mouth closed so nothing alive would fly into it.

After we stopped moving it took me a full thirty seconds of blinking and gasping to suddenly realize where we were. School, yes. I knew we were going to school. Sure. He'd said that, I'd agreed to it. I was on it. What I didn't expect was to be standing on the very edge of the soccer field, plastered to Levi's back, nose dripping mucus, while twenty guys moved around in various stages of practice. And that out of those twenty guys, at least twelve of them would manage to glance over right at the moment when I was trying to extract myself from my demon, sliding down his backside with zero grace and nearly toppling backward onto my own butt when he didn't release his grip on me right away.

And that one of those twelve guys staring at me would just happen to be Adam Birmingham. Lovely.

Out of breath from the ride, which made no sense since it

wasn't like *I* had exerted anything, I stood behind Levi and tugged down my hoodie, smoothed my hair, and mentally planned my escape route. If I just turned and walked straight to the west door of the building, I could be inside quickly, but I'd be in clear view of the practice for the entire trek. If I went south, I had tree coverage, but it would take longer. North, out of the question. I'd have to skirt the whole soccer field and that was a big no-thank-you.

Before I could decide on my cowardly retreat, a ball came toward us, arching up and spiraling fast. Letting out a squawk, I jumped back to dodge it, envisioning a broken nose, cracked skull, stinging hand, or any and all forms of pain and/or embarrassment. But Levi went up on his toes, stopped the ball's descent with his head, and bounced it gracefully to the ground. Dashing it back and forth with his feet, he then kicked it back on the field with a move that was World Cup worthy. Whoa. Impressed in spite of myself.

As was the West Shore soccer team. Three guys immediately jogged over and did the guy head nod, "Hey," thing.

"You from around here?" Adam—*my* Adam—asked.

"I just moved here," Levi said. "From Ontario. I'm actually here to register for school."

"Cool," Adam said. "You should talk to Coach Fowler, the dude over there in the black shirt. See about going out for the team. What position do you play?"

"Goalie."

"Cool. Hey, I'm Adam, this is Justin and Mack."

"Levi."

I was of course just standing there for the whole exchange of testosterone, staring at Adam discreetly—there is something so sexy about black soccer socks and cleats, though I could do without the baggy shorts—and not really paying attention to their conversation. Until Adam sort of leaned around Levi and looked right at me.

"Hi," he said.

"Hi," I chirped. No, I'm serious. I don't mean that as some cutesy dialogue tag. I actually chirped, like a swallow on helium.

Levi glanced over at me, his surprise at my ridiculous reaction clear on his face. His eyebrow went up. "This is Kenzie," he told Adam, obviously trying to gloss over the fact that I was standing there drooling mutely.

Somehow I found my voice—the real one, not the Tweetie version. "We actually know each other." Not as intimately as I wished, but there was an academic and daily relationship between us. "We're lab partners."

"We are?" Adam looked doubtful, his eyes raking over me.

Talk about being spanked. My mouth dropped. "Uh, yeah. Kenzie Sutcliffe. Seventh period, fetal pig next week . . ." I could feel my cheeks getting hot. He did not even recognize me? That was just so wrong.

"Oh, sure." Adam nodded, but I could tell he still lacked any sort of conviction that I wasn't totally lying to him. Like I had anything to gain by masterminding a deception regarding who sat where in A&P?

Tempted to shove my left arm at him and see if he at least recognized that, since that's the body part he usually spoke to across our lab desk, I gave an embarrassed smile. "Yeah, well, um."

"Did you do something different to your hair?" he asked, like this was the answer for why he had no memory of my face.

"*Yes*. Definitely. Totally different." Totally lying. My hair hadn't changed one flipping millimeter since June. I trimmed it, I dyed it, exactly the same every single time. But to spare us both further humiliation, I just went with it.

"I really like it this way," he said, a smile of relief crossing his face. "It goes with your eyes."

Huh. I so wanted that to be a compliment. It sounded like a compliment, in theory. But how exactly does dark brown hair with burgundy highlights go with blue-green eyes?

It doesn't, which is why Justin snorted to Adam's left and Levi frowned. Adam got a panicked look.

"Dude," he said to Levi, "Are you two like . . . together? I didn't mean anything by that, I was just saying . . ."

"No, we're not together," Levi scoffed.

Ouch. Not that I wanted to be with him either, but couldn't he have pretended for like two seconds that he totally wanted me so Adam would know I was highly sought after by at least one guy (demon)? And after I let him use my shower and feed off my envy, he couldn't even fake a crush on me? Yeesh.

"Kenzie is actually like my cousin. . . . Our moms have that thing, you know, where they've been friends since like preschool, and they feel like sisters, so they make us call them 'Aunt so and so,' and . . ." Levi's finger pointed from my chest to his. "They call us cousins."

Now that was a good cover story. Way better than actually being related to him.

"Oh." Adam nodded in understanding. "Cool. Hey, we'd better get back to practice. See you around." He smiled at me. Seriously. Right at me. Full white-teeth wattage. "Bye, Kenzie, see you tomorrow."

I nodded, forcing a weak lift of my own lips, my stomach up in my throat and my heart pounding like a snare drum. Adam spoke to me. Intentionally. This was good, right? Progress. Of a sort. As Levi and I walked away, I said, "Oh my God, he's not watching us, is he?" I mean, come on, I was wearing sweatpants. How cruel could fate be if he was checking out my butt when I was wearing faded navy cotton that drooped in unflattering places and had the word BECK (theater camp) marching across it?

Levi, demonic idiot, actually turned around to look behind us.

"Don't turn around! God!"

"He's not looking. Chill, babe." Levi shot me an amused look as my heart calmed down marginally. "You actually like that guy?"

"What do you mean?" I said, all fake innocence and wide eyes as we walked up the sidewalk to the side entrance of the building. "He's my lab partner and he seems nice."

"No, you *like* him, like him. You have the hots for him. You want to tonsil tango with Adam." He smirked and made kissy noises.

Irritated, I frowned at him. "How old are you, anyway? I would have thought demonic imprisonment would have matured you, regardless of your age. But obviously not." And it was all the more annoying that he had immediately guessed I had an inconvenient and unexplainable little crush on Adam.

"Well, I'm actually very young for a demon. I'm only five hundred and nineteen. And while we live in real time—you know, human time—we lose our long-term memories. Sort of like reverse Alzheimer's. They fade out to vague impressions and dreamlike images, so that I don't remember what I've been through or any 'life experiences.'" Levi made quote marks in the air. "So really, my maturity level is on the same level as a sixteen-year-old human male."

Wonderful. Just what we needed more of in the world.

"You don't remember your life? That sucks."

"Well, I remember a childhood, I remember growing up, then I remember being sixteen. . . . I have to stay sixteen because my job is to promote envy among teenagers. It's a pretty cushy position actually, because it's easy enough to push envy among American teens."

I could definitely see that. Talk about quick career advancement. He could scoot up that ladder an iPod at a time out in suburbia.

"But I must be maturing in spite of my hazy memories, because I started to realize what I was doing was wrong. That's when they tossed me in the portal."

Now that was really evil. Forced to stay at the same developmental phase indefinitely while encouraging others to be jerks or you get slapped in prison? Totally rude. Totally, well, demonic. Though I imagined it could have been worse. Being stuck as a teenager was way better than a perpetual eighty-five. Or picture being two and wearing a diaper forever. Yikes.

"What was prison like?"

Levi's expression changed. Most of the time, he looked casual, slightly amused, or irritated with me. But friendly enough. Normal.

Now he looked closed. Angry. Not nice. A little bit scary with those eyes narrowed and that black frown. And was I imagining it or did his pupils take on a deep red glow?

"I don't want to talk about it."

"Okay," I said quickly, freaked by that flare-up in his eyes. "That's cool. Sorry I brought it up, that was rude, because it's none of my business. Not anything I ever need to know, and obviously a painful subject for you. Forget I mentioned it. Reverse and erase. It's gone. I never brought it up."

Shoulders slumped, face resigned, he had opened the school

door and was waiting for me to walk through it, but I stopped and turned to him, feeling bad. Did he look a little sad? "But if you ever do want to talk about it, I'm a good listener. I can't promise to have all the answers, or even any of the answers, really, but I am very, very good at sympathizing, and just, well, listening. Being an ear. Which is probably why people tell me stuff, personal stuff, that maybe they really shouldn't, like my dental hygienist confessing she had an affair with her husband's brother. Why would she do that?" I shook my head. "I mean, just slap a sign on yourself that says 'I'm trying to ruin my marriage.' You know?"

Levi just looked at me, then he raised his arm, finger pointing into the school. "Get in there before I hurt you."

"Well." Giving a sniff, I tossed my hair back and walked through the door. "That's the last time I ever offer you a shoulder to cry on."

"Hallelujah," he muttered.

Ingrate.

But he nudged my shoulder, leaned down, mouth right by my ear, T-shirt brushing against my sleeve, and whispered, "Thanks, K. You're sweet, you know that?"

It was so unexpected that I felt my cheeks burn. "Whatever."

He laughed softly, and brushed his fingertips over my shoulder.

Did it feel good? Yeah. Was that bad? Oh, yeah, and then some.

Chapter Five

Demons can mind control. Who knew? But as I watched Levi chat with the school counselor, Mrs. Santana, I realized he was working some serious mojo on her. There was no other explanation for the way she just kept smiling and nodding and clicking on her computer.

In two-plus years I had never seen her so much as crack a single smile. And she didn't go to the restroom without proper paperwork. Yet she was letting Levi register for school with zero documentation, and a clearly BS story about hurricane damage, loss of records, blah, blah, blah. Yeah, because they're just ducking those hurricanes left and right in Ontario. Not to mention he should feel guilty for lying about something like that, which totally diminished what real hurricane victims went through.

Not looking the least bit guilty, he pulled out a driver's license and handed it to her. Where did he get *that*? And why didn't I have one? Grrr. Double grrr.

She glanced at it. "Perfect. I'll just make a copy of this. Now, do you want to take art?" she asked him, downright cheerful. "We can fit it in seventh period."

"If I take art, do I still have to take choir?"

"Nope. Art fulfills your Fine Arts requirement then."

"Cool, I'll do that."

Wait a minute. "You told me last year I couldn't take art until my senior year unless I planned to pursue art school. You said the course was restricted to students who needed to make a portfolio for college."

Her orange lips—do they honestly still sell orange lipstick?—squeezed together. "Kenzie, why don't you run along home while we finish up here. Or I think Coach Fowler could use an assistant on the soccer field. You could pick up the boys' balls."

Levi made a choking sound. I felt no urge to laugh. "That's okay. Levi wants me here, I'm sure, giving him advice. We're cousins, you know, and he's very shy."

She looked doubtful, but she let it drop. Fifteen minutes later we were walking out, Levi's schedule printed and in his hand. He had, by far, the easiest class load I had ever seen in my entire academic life. Starting the day with health, he moved to phys ed, then geometry, study hall, English, lunch, art, and child care.

"Child care?" I asked as we went down the hall in search of his locker assignment. I had a hard time picturing him in hot pursuit of a day-care career.

"Yep. It's a good way to meet chicks. Class will be loaded with them."

Nice.

"This sucks. You didn't have to take chemistry or government or anything. And that is so unfair that she's letting you take art."

"It's because I'm cute."

"It's because you brainwashed her."

"Jealous?" he asked, waving his schedule back and forth in front of my face.

Like I was going to fall for that. "No."

"Liar."

Totally. But I'd never admit it.

Levi may have brainwashed Mrs. Santana, but he had to have cloned my mother. There was no other explanation for why she agreed to let him stay with us based on a half-baked story that made no sense.

"So I just need a place to stay until the crew removes the black mold from our house. My parents want to be there to oversee the demolition and everything, but they want me gone."

"It doesn't sound safe for them to stay in that house." My

mother looked concerned as she put away groceries and handed two carrot sticks to Zoe to tide her over until dinner. "But of course you can stay with us. And if your parents need an attorney to consider their options with the builder, I can refer them to someone."

Naturally. I mentally rolled my eyes. My mother could litigate in her sleep.

"I guess everything's cool with that. . . . I'm not really sure. But thanks, though, I'll mention it to them." Levi held his hand out to Zoe and she coughed up one of her carrot sticks to him without a peep.

"We're happy to have you, Levi," my mother said with a smile. Lawyer lady, who asked three hundred thousand questions before I could leave the house to go the mall, and this was all she said? No phone call to Levi's parents? No background check?

Who were these people and where was my real family?

When my dad came home from Chicago at nine o'clock, we were playing Scrabble at the kitchen table. Levi was winning, Mom was laughing, Brandon was engaging in guy talk with his new demonic roommate, Zoe was sighing in adoration, passing over all her good letters to Levi, and I was pouting.

Life had gotten way too weird.

Dad just kissed Mom, glanced around the table, gave a mild wave to everyone, ruffled Zoe's hair, and told Levi, "I didn't know Kenzie had a new boyfriend. Nice to meet you."

Clueless. Totally clueless. All of them. Though Dad got

points for saying "new boyfriend," which implied Levi had had oodles of predecessors.

"I'm going to bed," I said, pushing my tiles over to Brandon.

Note: No one tried to stop me from leaving the room. I wasn't exactly Sunny Scrabble Player.

A headache was stabbing at my eyes and I felt like my body had disconnected from my brain. The day needed to end before I cracked, so I climbed up the stairs and went into my bathroom to collect my toiletries. It was going to be awkward to explain to my mother why I was borrowing Zoe and Brandon's bathroom, but maybe she wouldn't notice. Then again, maybe if I just washed my face and brushed my teeth really fast, I could put off moving my stuff until the morning. Carting away my makeup and all my various lotions and sprays and products seemed like too much work.

I was wetting a washcloth, with cleansing facial scrub on my face, when I heard the drain in my bathtub burp. Like water had gurgled back out of the drain and into the shower. Probably not a big deal. Probably just some backup, or maybe Mom was running the dishwasher and it had tossed some air pressure my pipe's way. Maybe.

Leaning over tentatively, cloth in hand, I tried to peek around the shower curtain, which was pulled back to the left, blocking the view of the drain. What would have been the logical thing to do here? Run, right? Yeah, you would think. Not what I did, because clearly I am not logical.

Normally I'm not the least bit brave either, but the fear of humiliation was greater than the fear of otherworldly creatures. Having Levi smirk at me if I came flying out of the bathroom over less than nothing seemed infinitely more horrifying than what I might actually find. Besides, it was just a little noise, not enough of a rustle back there to be a full-fledged beast or man-sized demon. Convinced I was being a total wimp, I yanked the curtain back.

The bottom of my bathtub was vicious red, a liquid pool darkening around the drain, bubbling and sending sprays of sticky fluid up onto the walls. Bad enough that it looked like a body had been drained of blood in my shower, but what really freaked me out was the very clear—I'm not making this up, swear—outline of a man's face in the liquid. It looked like someone had taken a finger and sketched out a head, eyes, a nose, lips and everything.

And then it growled at me.

Okay, I was out. I screamed.

Afraid to turn my back on whatever it was, I scooted back, back, back, tripping over the towel still lying there from that morning, and stumbled over the doorjamb. Hands touched my shoulders—so not fair that somehow it still got behind me—and I spun around, lashing out, figuring if I was going to go down, I should at least make an effort to maim the mutant from the underworld that was attacking me.

This mutant had a familiar voice. "Calm down," Levi said,

pushing my hands straight down by my hips and setting me aside so he could enter the bathroom. "What did you see?"

Calming down. Sure. Absolutely. I was on it. I sucked in a breath and crept back into the room behind him. "In the tub," I whispered.

"What was it?" he whispered back, glancing at me.

"Red stuff, bloody, almost, a face . . ."

"Why are we whispering?" Levi said, his voice mocking.

Hey, I was proud of myself that I was still standing there— even if I was holding on to his arms to use him like a shield if anything came rising out from the bowels of hell into my shower—and he was complaining about my projection?

"Aren't you worried something is wrong?"

"I've got it under control." Levi pulled back the curtain and surveyed the scene, then leaned over the tub and started speaking some freaky foreign language. I think it was Latin, but really, when have I heard Latin? It just sounded like it should be Latin.

A growling sound startled me and I clung to Levi, trying to look both out of morbid curiosity and the feeling that I should be aware if something flew up and at me, and yet not really wanting to see too much. There was a *pop*, and all the red swirled right back down the drain, leaving a very disgusting slimy coating. It made one last snarling protest, baring its gelatinous teeth at the tip of the drain, before disappearing.

"What was *that*?"

"Prison guard projecting himself. Sort of like a hologram . . . He was testing the portal and checking for my presence."

"So you just gave yourself away, that can't be good." I gnawed on my fingernail and frowned at the bloody ring in my tub. Who was going to clean that?

"What's the matter?" my father called from the bottom of the stairs, not really sounding all that concerned. I could have been murdered three times over and my parents would accuse me of drama.

"Spider," I yelled back. "Levi got it, thanks."

"Then tell him to get out of your bathroom. And you'd better be dressed or I'm coming up there to haul him out myself."

I rolled my eyes, even if he couldn't see me. "Dad, it's not like that. We're just friends."

"But we could be so much more." Levi raised his eyebrow up and down and did that lip-smacking, stupid-guy thing.

In his demon dreams. "I'm going to bed."

Three days. That's how long it took for Levi Athan (what kind of last name was that anyway?) to become the new It Guy at West Shore High School. Three days and everyone knew his name, from senior football player to the lowest freshman. I had been at that school for more than two years and ninety percent of the student body had no clue who I was.

Yet Levi just waltzed in with his cake schedule and his demon-generated driver's license and he was suddenly all that. His table was full at lunch. The soccer team high-fived him in the hall. Girls, normal girls who should know better, like my best friend Isabella, giggled vapidly and found reasons to bend over when he walked by.

Walking beside him when we got to school in the morning was nausea-inducing.

"Hi, Levi." Hair flip from Harriet.

"Hey, hot stuff." Sultry smile from Savannah.

"Morning, Levi." Giggle from Grace.

Gag, gag, gag.

The constant *ding, ding, ding* of his cell phone announcing a text message was like fingernails on a chalkboard, and I tried not to pout as I wondered exactly how had this happened??

What had I done to deserve this? Not only was I kicked out of my own bathroom indefinitely (as the potential for growling bloody faces to appear was huge), I also had to be subjected to the sight of every person I knew falling for the charm of a demon with big feet. After thinking, sort of, in a weird not-getting-enough-sleep kind of way, that maybe he had been flirting with me.

Not that I'd want him to. I mean, he was a demon. But I had thought maybe he was, and that was kind of a cool thing, you know, ego flattering. Only now he was demonstrating daily that it had been absolutely entirely my imagination since I was forced to watch him flirting in actuality with a dozen girls. Sometimes all at once.

Worse yet, they'd started calling my house. And randomly appearing in my driveway, where they hovered around like remora with a shark, turning every way he turned, hoping for social scraps.

They said things like, "Why does that girl live in your house?"

"Does that girl go to our school? I think I saw her in detention."

Hello, *my* house, and I hadn't had a detention since I got busted for gum chewing in seventh grade. Yeah. That Girl was me. They would point or nod their heads toward me and lower their voices like I was too special needs to figure out they were talking about me.

Grace and Savannah fell in step beside us on Friday, keeping up a constant chatter. I fell back. Fringe. Yet again. That was me. But I really didn't want to be part of his harem either, and Savannah's steady dialogue on how many friends she had on her MySpace page was eye-rolling, tear-my-hair, choking-gag, slit-my-wrists boring. The probability of me whining was huge, so I kept my mouth clamped shut.

When I broke away for real, Levi noticed and gave me a smile and a wave. "See you after school, K."

"Is she your little sister?" Grace asked.

"More like personal assistant," Levi said, with a backward grin at me.

Oh, we needed to have a serious talk.

While Levi was taxing his brain in child care, I was sweating my way through a pop quiz in anatomy & physiology. Why was it I could remember three-page monologues but not a few lousy science definitions? It defied logic, but it was true. I confused all my genuses and species and always put the life cycle completely out of order, calling into question our very existence if evaporation came prior to rainfall. This was why I was in Science for Dummies, the three-year track designed for those of us who didn't need advanced courses for college, and would unintentionally blow up the lab if allowed to take chemistry. And physics? Forget it. I couldn't even spell it. But I should have been able to pass one lousy A&P class.

Given all the shifting he was doing next to me, Adam wasn't having much luck with the essay quiz either.

"Time's up. Pass them forward," Mr. Beckner said.

"Damn," Adam muttered under his breath.

I glanced over at his paper and saw half of it was still blank. "Sorry," I told him in sympathy, taking his test and stacking it with mine. I poked Rachel Gibbs in the arm to get her attention and handed them forward to her.

"Hey, uh . . ." Adam said, pulling his long legs in under the table, then jutting them out again.

"Yeah?" I said, hoping he was talking to me. No one else appeared to be aware of him at the moment, but he wasn't really looking at me either. It could go either way.

But he was talking to me because he glanced up briefly and said, "So, uh, Kenzie, how about you and me go to homecoming?"

Excuse me? Total shift of the planet on its axis. I was either hallucinating, or the world as I knew it had come to an end, or Adam Birmingham had seen the light and just invited me to a formal dance with him.

"What?" I said, licking my lips nervously. Why was my fantasy suddenly springing to life? Stuff like that just didn't happen. Not to me.

Adam, who had never so much as glanced my way in the seven weeks we'd been sitting next to each other in class; who had proclaimed he didn't even know my name, or that I was his lab partner; and who could get any girl in the junior class he wanted (Well, almost any girl. Amber Janson and a few others were probably technically above his reach.), was suddenly interested in ME?

Call me a cynic, but nothing just magically changes in the blink of an eye and you get what you want, unless you win the lottery.

"I thought we could go to the dance," he repeated. "Together."

He gave a nervous smile, his pretty, white teeth flashing at me. "We'll hang out."

We'll hang out. Huh. Before I started mentally shopping for my dress, I couldn't help but blurt out, "Why?"

Way to flirt, Kenzie.

"What do you mean?" Now he pulled his legs back and cleared his throat.

"I mean, why did you ask me?" Just let it go, let it go, I told myself, yet I had the nagging suspicion that this wasn't normal, business-as-usual behavior. That something had motivated Adam "Don't Speak" Birmingham to unglue his lips and invite me to homecoming. Where people would see us. Together.

"Do you have another date or something? If you do, that's cool. Just thought I'd ask." He was starting to sound uncomfortable.

"Do you like me?" I have no clue why I said that. It was like a freak had taken over my body and wanted to humiliate me and ruin the greatest chance for romance I'd ever stumbled across. Or it was pride, the certainty that Adam didn't like me, the girl he hadn't even noticed. I wasn't about to be the butt of some stupid soccer joke.

"Sure, I like you. You have nice . . . eyes. And Levi said you're cool."

Oh, here we go. "What did Levi tell you about me?"

"Nothing, just that you're cool, and I should ask you to the dance, and we could all go together. . . ."

"No talking!" Mr. Beckner yelled at us.

My stomach sank. "Oh," I said. "He asked you to ask me, didn't he?" Adam was trying to get on Levi's good side, and for whatever reason, Levi had pressured him. It was obvious to me, especially when Adam didn't answer me, but instead turned to the front of the room, his hand clenching his pencil tightly.

"So is that a no?" he asked in a low voice a minute later when the teacher's back was to us.

"I don't know," I said honestly. "Let me think about it."

Who would have thought that would come out of my mouth? But it did, and I was grateful he let it drop.

I was embarrassed, feeling like I didn't want to go out with a guy who had no real interest in me. That smacked of pure desperation, and while I was many things, desperate wasn't one of them. I could leave the dance as easily as I could take it, and it was no big deal. I would live. Nothing was worth being a sympathy date.

On the other hand. Maybe Adam really did like me. Maybe all Adam had needed was a nudge and some persuasion from Levi. It could happen. Who's to say what was really going on in the strange inner-workings of Adam's mind?

Time to hit pause and think it through before I gave him an answer.

I really didn't want to throw away the opportunity to make out with him in formal wear just yet.

Chapter Six

"You have some explaining to do," I told Levi after we shook off the last of the female fluff clinging to him and entered my house after school.

"What now?" He rolled his eyes.

Nice. And after I was lying to my own flesh and blood to let him stay in my house.

"Adam Birmingham invited me to homecoming today."

"Cool. Now you can get a hot dress with cleavage and let him ram his tongue down your throat."

Levi dropped his backpack and went straight for our refrigerator, stepping over Zoe's elaborate Polly Pocket setup. It looked like Polly was going for a good horseback ride at the stables after a hard time shopping at the boutique. That was the life.

"Do you happen to know anything about why Adam invited me?" And was Levi being sarcastic or was that actual disgust?

"Why would I?" His head disappeared into the fridge. For being a demon who fed off envy, he could consume an awful lot of chips and soft drinks.

"Because he mentioned that you mentioned that maybe he should ask me."

He didn't reply, just reappeared with a Coke.

"So, just for future reference, I don't really like the idea that I need you twisting guys' arms to get me a date. I'd rather stay home and knit than be a pity date."

With a snort, he popped the top on his can. "You, knitting? Yeah, okay."

"Levi . . ."

"Fine, so I suggested he ask you. Look, I didn't want you home alone. It could be dangerous. And I know you like Adam— though why is anyone's guess, because he's about as interesting as a doorknob, but I figured this way you're with someone, you're having fun, you're safe."

"Adam is way more interesting than a doorknob." Possibly. I didn't really know that for a fact, today's conversation being the longest we'd ever had. But he didn't look doorknob dull. Just quiet. Maybe. But what did Levi have against him anyway?

"Not who I would have chosen for you, but hey, everyone's entitled to like who they want." He chugged his drink.

"Who would you choose for me?" Not that I cared. Much.

I expected him to name someone off the wall. But he just glanced over at me, eyes dark, expression enigmatic. "Someone who would appreciate you more than Adam will."

It was a nothing of an answer, and his criticism of Adam felt like an insult to me. I unzipped my backpack and pulled out my iPod. "Yeah, and who are you taking to homecoming?"

"Amber Janson."

"Amber?!? But she's with Logan." Not to mention that Levi was, well, Levi—not really good-looking at all—and Amber was born without a single physical flaw.

Levi gave me a smug smile. "Not anymore."

That was too much for me. I stuck my earbuds in, forgetting entirely that I wanted to talk to him about my bathroom and how we were going to close the portal so I could resume normal life activities. "Well, have fun. Try to get a word in edgewise when she spends the whole night blabbing about herself."

"Meow."

I reached down and picked up one of Polly's skirts, the old rubber kind, before Polly went click-on. I threw it at Levi. Not that a dime-sized pink rubber skirt was any sort of weapon. It barely skimmed his arm before dropping to the floor.

Ugly, jealous feelings that I hated and didn't entirely understand swelled up in me, and I left the room feeling mean and confused, and not at all pleasant.

"Thanks for the after-school snack," Levi called.

Ugh. I turned on my iPod and stomped upstairs.

* * *

"Adam asked you to homecoming and you said you'd think about it?" Isabella gaped at me, her hand frozen on her knee where she'd been tugging up her pink tights. "Have you completely lost your mind?"

It felt that way. That my mind had suddenly snapped and collapsed in on itself. It was the most plausible explanation for why I hadn't leaped up on my desk and shrieked *yes, yes, yes* when Adam invited me.

"It made sense at the time," I said.

I was at the theater for my part-time job answering the phones and taking ticket sales. Isabella had advanced ballet classes five days a week so she was always there too. She was on a water break and I had just told her the news.

"How could that possibly make sense? Nothing about that could ever make sense." She was so indignant she had both hands out in disgust. "You have to call him tonight. Right now. You have to tell him you'll go."

"But . . . the thing is, Levi made him ask me. Do you know how lame that makes me feel? Like a charity date."

Her eyebrow went up. "So? Guys are stupid. They don't notice anything. And sometimes they need someone else to point out that there is a perfect match for them right in front of their face. You should be grateful to Levi for saving you the hassle of having to throw yourself at Adam."

Well, there was always that. "I never would have thrown my-self at Adam." I swiveled back and forth on my office chair, looking at Isabella over the reception counter.

"Exactly. Which is why Levi is now responsible for securing your complete and total happiness. What a thoughtful guy. Like I said, you should be grateful."

Yeah, that's what I was feeling. Not.

"So call Adam. Now. While I'm standing here."

"No!" *I* didn't even want to hear what I was going to say. I sure as heck didn't want her witnessing it too.

"Call him or I'll call him for you."

"What are we, twelve?"

"Exactly." She gave me a triumphant smile. "Call him, K. This is what you've wanted for like a year." With a finger wave and a leg leap, she was gone.

Leaving me with the phone. I picked it up. Put it down. Sucked in a breath. Cursed myself for being a wimp. Felt a hot, nasty sweat break out on my forehead. Wondered why I cared so much. Knew I could never do it.

What was the worst that could happen? Adam could say he'd changed his mind because I'd acted like a psycho freak when he'd asked me. Which would be reasonable. It probably hadn't been easy for him to ask me in the first place and I'd gone off on him, all "why are you asking me?" I'd broken the rules of flirta-tion by saying exactly what was on my mind.

Which should be okay. Seriously. Why *couldn't* I say what I was thinking? The last thing in the world I wanted was to be fake with a guy, letting him fall for someone who didn't exist instead of the real me.

Girl power, man, I was on it.

I picked up the phone, closed my eyes, and dialed. Yes, I knew the number by heart. Is that sick or what?

"Hello?" a woman said.

"Hi, could I speak to Adam please?" He wasn't home, I just knew it, and I didn't have his cell phone number. Or his e-mail address. E-mail would have been so much easier. Maybe I could hang up and search to see if he had a MySpace page. Why communicate live when we could do it electronically? That way he couldn't hear my voice trembling.

"He's not here."

Both wildly relieved and yet horrified that I couldn't actually get the conversation over with, I rubbed my eyes. This was just embarrassing. I had somehow regressed to fifth grade.

"Can I take a message?" His mother sounded mildly curious, but, unlike my parents, was taking the high road and not asking seventy-five ultra-personal questions.

"Could you just tell him Kenzie called? Thanks."

I hung up the phone and laid my head down on the desk. Total. Loser. When did this happen? I needed therapy.

"Hey, Kenzie, what's up?"

Lifting my head from the desk, I gave Tyler Matthews a weak smile. He worked part-time at the theater too, in janitorial.

I knew him because he'd done tech for the show *The Secret Garden*. "Hey, Tyler."

"You trying out for *A Midsummer Night's Dream*?"

"Yes." Auditions were the following week and I hadn't even read the thing, let alone worked on a monologue. I was too busy answering the phone for Levi and trekking my clothes down the hall to shower.

Tyler jingled his keys in his hand. "I'm off for the night. You need a ride home?"

Okay, this was a new suggestion. Usually I had to wait for Isabella to get out of dance, which meant waiting around for an hour after my shift ended, which, generally speaking, sucked. Tyler had never offered me a ride home before. I looked at him, trying to decide if this was a sudden attack of niceness—I've heard that exists in guys—or if he was working up to hitting on me.

Like I had any clue how to interpret a guy. Tyler wasn't even looking at me, but at his keys as he flung them around. He didn't look particularly brimming with lust or anything though, so it seemed safe to say yes. "Sure, that'd be great. Let me tell Isabella I'm not waiting for her."

Leaning over, I picked up my backpack and turned the phones on to night service. I stood up and came around the desk to head for the dance studio. Suddenly there was a hand on the small of my back. Hello. Strange appendage touching me. I walked forward quickly, out of his touch, sort of annoyed. What gave him the idea that he could just touch me?

Of course, maybe he was just being thoughtful. Gentlemanly or something. It wasn't like where he'd touched or how he'd touched had been inappropriate, just unexpected. Polite. Thoughtful, definitely—that was it.

Five minutes later, in the car with his hand on my knee, I kind of got the feeling thoughtfulness wasn't first and foremost on his brain.

"What are you doing?" I asked, picking up his hand with both of mine and tossing it back toward him. I've noticed I don't do subtle very well.

Tyler is a good-looking guy, with longish sandy-colored hair and a nice sense of rocker style. Pretty smile. Decent build. But obviously dumb as a fence post if he thought that, without any warning or flirting or clue from me of a mutual like-thing, he could just toss his hand in my lap and have me fall down in gratitude.

We were driving on the highway. Where did he think we were going to go from there?

Guys should be given a manual at age ten on how to be even remotely attractive to girls and women, and number six could be: "Do not engage in random and ill-timed groping."

Glancing over at me, he tried to move his hand back into my personal space. "I thought maybe we could go to the park. . . . I know you've been checking me out for weeks, and you should know, I feel the same way."

Oooo-kay.

"Tyler, I don't want to go to the park." And really, even if I had liked Tyler in an amorous way—which I didn't—I'm sorry, but a trip to the park after zero conversation, no instant messaging, no e-mails, no movie dates, no hanging out, no burgers-and-fries dinners . . . that was just assuming way too much. Hey, I like you, so let's go mess around in my Honda Civic? Wow. That was the basis for a beautiful relationship.

"You have to get home? Just call your mom and tell her you'll be late."

It was amazing how he could drive stick shift with his right hand making inroads to my thigh, but the lack of changing gears in highway driving was probably assisting him in multi-tasking. I knew the mechanics of driving. Knew how to drive. Just didn't have a license, which was of course the reason I was stuck in the car with testosterone-soaked Tyler.

"I don't *have* to go home, I *want* to go home. I'm not interested in the park. It's not my thing, okay?" I tossed his hand off for the second time. "Watch the fingers, Matthews. I'm serious."

We were now off the highway, so he did actually need his hand to downshift. But he still glanced over at me. "Are you sure you want to go home?" he asked, like I was turning down something really good, like a chocolate-sprinkle-covered donut or a twenty lying on the ground.

"Yeah. Positive." Quite sure I wasn't going to go home and writhe in regret.

"I didn't realize you were so uptight."

"Well, now you know." We were pulling into my driveway, which was a little frightening in and of itself. I had not told Tyler where I lived. I was positive he had never been to my house before. He didn't even go to the same high school as me, but was one suburb east of mine. There was no way he should know where I lived.

Heart rate picking up in pace, I discreetly reached for the door handle, looking to hop out the second the car stopped. I opened my mouth to give a polite thanks for the ride, only to find I couldn't speak because Tyler's lips were suddenly smothering mine.

Hello. Gagging. Not prepared, I just clamped my mouth closed as I tried to maneuver backward away from him. Getting a hand between us, I shoved on his chest, which was damp with sweat. Eew. Tyler didn't retreat even an inch, and I simultaneously pushed him while turning my head to break the contact. His head just followed mine, which was irritating.

Legs and knees were ineffectual given our position in the car, so I was raising my hand to nail Tyler on the side of his skull when the passenger door flew open. Lurching sideways, I almost spilled out onto the driveway, but it was worth it to get away from Tyler, who was still pursuing me, his skin clammy and covered in sweat, his eyes glazed over with . . . desire? Sick. He looked so wild, I could hardly believe he was the mild-mannered janitor who pushed his broom with zero ambition.

He was breathing hard and actually shaking a little, so focused on me, so out of control yet determined, it was terrifying. Fear had me frozen, hanging on to the door, staring up at him for a split second, totally and completely weirded out. I had been more annoyed than scared until I caught a glimpse of him, and now I suddenly had no clue what to do.

But then Tyler was off me, his back flying into the glass on the driver's side. The sound of the crash and Tyler's groan as he hit sent me into action. Rolling onto my stomach, I scrambled out of the car in a frantic crabwalk, crawling right past a pair of legs in jeans. Levi. I should have known it was Levi rescuing me.

Which would have been comforting if I hadn't looked up and seen that Levi's eyes were glowing a scarlet red in the dark. That was nice and demonic. Red eyes. Up on my knees now, I paused and looked over my shoulder to really check those suckers out. Whoa. Then survival instincts kicked in and I climbed to my feet to run.

Just in time to turn and see Tyler's foot come flying out and nail Levi in the chest.

Dude. That had to hurt.

And I was losing my mind because I was actually starting to use the word *dude* internally.

I must have made some kind of noise because Levi said in a low, angry voice, his hand rubbing his ribs, "Go into the house, Kenzie."

That would have been smart. You didn't need to be in the

National Honor Society to figure that one out. But I was too shocked to do much more than just stand there, mouth open, tugging my T-shirt back into place.

So I had a really good view when Levi reached out, grabbed Tyler's outstretched foot, and wrenched it to the left so hard I heard Tyler's jeans tear and a curse fly out of his mouth.

Startled, I jumped a little and edged backward toward the front walk. Okay, something wasn't right here. "Levi, it's okay, he didn't really do anything. . . . I mean, you stopped him in time. Don't . . ." Trash his wardrobe. *Break his bones*. Not that I was feeling much sympathy for Tyler, but Levi getting thrown in juvenile hall for assault didn't seem like a good plan either. He'd just left prison. I didn't want to be responsible for sending him back. And I didn't think lack of adequate hygiene would be his biggest concern in a mortal prison full of gang members, drug pushers, and murderers.

"You don't know what he is, Kenzie. Get in the house."

I knew he was a seriously presumptuous and oversexed jerk, but I just wanted him gone, not a battle for my honor in the driveway when my parents might stroll out to investigate at any moment. As it was, Mrs. Lawson from across the street was probably rubbernecking, catching the whole scene with the night-vision goggles she'd bought her daughter after seeing *Spy Kids*.

But any answer I might have given evaporated when Tyler catapulted forward like a pouncing lion and cracked his skull against Levi's in a move that rivaled the WWE. Owww.

"She's mine, demon," Tyler said as they fell to the ground, rolling and punching and kicking.

Excuse me? His? And did he just say demon?

Levi growled, baring his teeth at Tyler. "Touch her again and I'll rip you into pieces."

Growling is not normal. It brought to mind the face in my bathtub, and the horrible truth that no matter how dorky and human he seemed, Levi was a demon. I hadn't exactly forgotten that little fact, but this just really drove it home.

Not to mention I didn't know what Tyler was, but it was starting to become obvious he wasn't just the pervert boy next door.

"Levi . . ." I said, not sure why. But I was standing there wondering what I was supposed to do. Call the cops? Scream? Vanquish Tyler with a curse or something?

He didn't answer me because he and Tyler were doing that rolling around on the ground guy thing, grappling at each other's throats and trying to get in punches. Neither seemed to be winning, and neither seemed to really be in any sort of danger of injury.

"Um . . ." I watched for another minute, fear shifting to annoyance. How long were they going to do this? "Just let him go, Levi. It's cold out here."

Ignoring me, Levi got on top of Tyler and cracked his head down onto the concrete. It hit so hard I gasped as Tyler groaned, and I started forward, not wanting Levi to kill Tyler. Not that

I felt tons of sympathy for Tyler, but death sounded messy and complicated and altogether too final. The guy didn't deserve to die, so I had to break this up. But then I saw Tyler's eyes were glowing in the dark too, his a deep vibrant purple, as he gave a wince of pain and sank backward. Great. I had two demons in the driveway.

"Uncle," Tyler said.

"Thought so." Levi definitely sounded smug as he peeled himself off Tyler and got to his feet.

Uncle? Demons made each other cry uncle?

Tyler stood up too, shook out his legs, and dusted off his butt. "Sorry, Kenzie," he said with a shrug. "Maybe we can hang out another time."

I didn't think so. And that didn't exactly sound like an apology for pawing me, but more like a sorry that he got interrupted. "Tyler, you totally crossed the line. I told you I wasn't interested and you pushed way too far. I don't ever want to *hang out* with you again. In fact, I want an apology and then I want you to turn around and find a new hall to sweep the next time we're in the same room at the Beck."

They both stared at me like I'd spoken in ancient Arabic.

"What?" I demanded.

"You mean you weren't like totally into Tyler?" Levi asked, rubbing his hand over his hair.

How was that news? "No. That sort of explains why I was shoving him off me and trying to get the car door open."

"You were?" Tyler asked, looking puzzled. "But . . . that doesn't make any sense."

Because it was so unusual for a girl to turn him down? Please. I gave a heavy eye roll. Tyler and Levi just looked at each other, their animosity seemingly forgotten. Tyler glanced over at me, his eyes—thankfully no longer purple but a standard brown—going wide.

"Whoa, dude, now I get it. Okay, sorry Kenzie." He slammed the passenger door shut and went around to the driver's side. "I'm out of here. See you around, Leviathan."

As Tyler peeled out, his car bouncing on the curb, I turned to Levi, the hairs on the back of my neck raised. "Leviathan? *Leviathan?* Who the heck is Leviathan? And isn't that like Satan's nickname or something?"

"I'm Leviathan," he said, rolling his eyes right back at me. "Duh."

Chapter Seven

Well, that was just wrong. "So are you telling me you're Satan?" I squeaked, taking a tiny step backward.

"Don't be overdramatic. I'm not Satan. I'm a demon. We've been through all that. And the first Leviathan is not Satan either, but the demon in charge of the deadly sin envy." Levi shrugged. "I'm named after him. . . . It's kind of like a godfather sort of thing."

"My godfather is my uncle Jim and he's a podiatrist in Vermilion. It's not normal to have a fallen angel for a godfather. It's just not." In case he didn't know that.

"It is where I come from. And were you serious when you said that you weren't really like, um, responding to Tyler?"

"Responding to Tyler?" I got indignant all over again.

"Hardly. He basically attacked me with wet lips and octopus arms. I am actually grateful you showed up when you did. He was shaking and sweating . . . it was disgusting." I shuddered at the memory. It had been more than a little creepy, and it had bothered me how truly unprepared I'd been to deal with him. I wasn't sure what would have happened if Levi hadn't come outside.

"But . . ." Levi shook his head. "Tyler is a demon from the Lust sect."

That rolled around in my head. Suddenly the shaking and ashen face made sense. I recognized the symptoms from Levi. "Are you saying he was hungry? And that if I had *responded*, it would have fed him?"

"Yeah. And the thing is, Tyler doesn't have to work at it at all. He's powerful enough that all girls are attracted to him. So he's pretty lazy in his methods."

That explained the complete lack of pre-flirting. "Well, *I'm* not attracted to him. At all. And if he ever tries to cram his tongue in my mouth again, I'll bite it off."

"Huh."

There was a lot left unsaid in that word. "What does that mean?"

"Nothing. It's just . . . nothing."

I had started to walk toward the front door of my house, but I stopped, tucking my hair behind my ears. "Tell me, Levi. It's been a lousy day and I'm completely out of patience." And suddenly I sounded like my mother. Next I'd be wagging my finger at him.

Biting his fingernail, Levi studied the straw bale my mom had set next to the walkway with a half dozen pumpkins surrounding it. He plucked at the straw. "It's just that the only girls who don't fall under Tyler's little lust mojo are girls who are already taken."

"I'm not taken." I wish.

"But your destiny must already be determined. You've already met your mate."

"My mate? I don't want a mate! I just want a date for homecoming." I frantically tugged at the strings on my hoodie. "Levi . . . this is just crazy. I don't know anyone who could possibly be my mate." Unless it was Adam. Which frankly seemed so very unlikely. "And I'm too young to mate anyway." Just the word alone was giving me convulsions. It sounded so Animal Planet.

"Maybe *mate* isn't the right word," he said. "But you know, someone you're in love with, or might be in love with soon, and vice versa. On a permanent lifetime basis."

"You're talking about marriage." The whole front yard spun and I swear I saw black spots in front of my eyes. "I don't even have my driver's license yet, I cannot *think* about getting married."

"You know what, just forget about it. It probably doesn't mean anything. Maybe Tyler was too hungry and he didn't have his usual charm."

"Okay, I'll forget it." But I knew he was just saying that to prevent a total meltdown on my part. And I was going to have a hard time forgetting the fact that demons thought I'd already met the guy I was supposed to mate. Marry. Fall in love with. A long time from now. Hopefully. Just because I knew him didn't mean the whole head-over-heels thing was going to happen anytime soon. People sometimes know each other in high school, go off to college, meet back up at their ten-year reunion, and fall in love despite never having glanced at each other even once back in the day. Probably that was exactly what was going to happen with me.

I was almost maybe sure of it.

When we went into the house, Zoe was standing in front of my parents in the family room in her bubblegum-pink peignoir pajama set, arms crossed over her chest. Mom and Dad looked mildly amused, while Zoe looked downright indignant.

"I do deserve more allowance," she said, leaning forward aggressively. "I get a dollar a week, and that's what you gave Kenzie when she was five and that's not fair."

Her logic sounded whack to me but I figured it was none of my business. I was halfway up the stairs when I realized Levi was hovering on the bottom step. "What?" I asked him.

He just shook his head, clearly listening to their conversation.

My dad told Zoe, "That is fair. You both got the same amount when you were five."

"But stuff costs more now so my dollar can't buy me as much. So it's not fair. That's what Levi said."

Horrified, I glared at him. He was manipulating a five-year-old. "You're evil," I told him.

But he just shrugged and gave me a grin. "It's true. Your

buck ten years ago went a lot farther than poor Zoe's dollar to-day. The kid's getting ripped off, as I explained to her."

"Yeah, and the fact that you just fed off of a five-year-old's envy still makes you evil." I rubbed my elbow where it had slammed into the car door when I'd fallen out onto the drive-way. "I'm going to bed. And I don't want to hear the *D* word for at least twenty-four hours."

"What's the *D* word? Dude? Dessert? Diamonds? Donkey?"

"Demon, you dork. I don't want to hear anything about demons." Not only did I not want to talk about them, I wanted to forget they existed altogether.

"You know, we should talk about what might have happened if I wasn't there and you weren't somehow immune to Tyler's, you know, talents."

That was the last thing in the world I wanted to talk about. "It doesn't matter because I am immune to him." I had a thought. "Hey, is Ben Jacobs a demon?"

"Never heard of him."

Levi made like he was going to follow me into my bedroom, but I stuck my arm out and blocked him. "Your room is down the hall."

"We're talking," he protested, looking mortally wounded. "And why do you think Ben Jacobs is a demon? Maybe I should check him out."

"I wondered if he had the same ability as Tyler, because Ben is a complete freak with bad teeth and a fake gangsta wardrobe and no conversational skills whatsoever, yet he has a steady stream of attractive girlfriends. It defies all logic."

But Levi shook his head. "No, he can't be a demon. Only one from each sect can be in a fifty-mile radius, at bare minimum. Sometimes way broader depending on the population."

"So you're saying Tyler is responsible for encouraging teenage lust all over the west side of Cleveland?"

He nodded.

Huh. "And yet he doesn't seem at all ambitious. Amazing. Can I go to bed now?"

"Chill out. It's like nine o'clock. You can't be that tired. We need to talk about the portal."

No, no, no. I leaned against my door frame and sighed. "Do we have to go there? I just want to put on fluffy pajamas and read a magazine in bed. Maybe the portal will just go away on its own."

Levi snorted. "Yeah, that's realistic. Look, I did some research, and in the underworld we place our prisons in so-called secret locations, but everyone knows they're at points where the latitude and longitude intersect with a six, or with a derivative of six in the coordinates."

"Of course." I yawned. If he got mathematical with me, I was going to fall asleep standing up. I don't do formulas.

"Each prison is shaped like a pentagram, with the five principal prisons forming a larger pentagram. If my calculations are correct, then your bathroom is directly above the left corner of my prison, the point that connects it to the other prisons in the pentagram."

Oh, lovely.

"So when you dropped your 'lotion' . . ." he made very sarcastic quote marks in the air, "you opened the portal that has always existed."

I rubbed my temples. "And how did you figure this out?" Surely he was wrong. I couldn't have been showering on top of a demon portal for the past five years.

"Calculus. Jeannie Sharpton did most of it for me." He winked. "She's got quite a brain in her head."

"You told her you're a demon?" For some weird reason, I was hurt. I thought his demonic status was our little secret, sort of like an inside joke.

"No, how stupid do I look?"

"Do you really want me to answer that?"

He got a funny look on his face. "Kenzie . . ."

"What?" My heart started to pound as he lifted his hand. He looked serious. He looked worried. Like he was going to tell me something awful, I could just feel it. Or even worse, he almost looked like he was going to kiss me. Which I didn't want him to do, of course. Honestly.

But he just popped his finger on my nose—I absolutely despise when people do that—and said, "Don't project. It's okay that Jeannie is smarter than you. We all have our special talents and, repeat after me here, 'My name is Kenzie and I like myself.'"

It's a miracle I didn't beat him senseless, but I was exhausted and Zoe interrupted us by bounding up the stairs, looking triumphant. She strutted her little self up to Levi.

"It worked," she said. "I asked for two dollars, and they said no, but they gave me a dollar and fifty cents instead."

"Alright." Levi stuck his hand out and Zoe gave him a high five, grinning for all she was worth.

"How long are you gonna live with us?" she asked him.

I was wondering the same thing myself.

"Why?" he asked. "You want me to leave?" He rubbed her head in a teasing gesture that sent her rocking back and forth.

"No!" she shouted, because Zoe isn't known for being subtle. "I want you to stay forever. And if you marry Kenzie, you can."

How did she pull *that* out of her kindergarten behind? "I don't think so," I said, horrified, Levi's earlier words strolling through my brain.

Levi frowned at me briefly before he gave Zoe a charming smile. "I'd rather wait and marry you."

I gave him points for defusing what was a monumentally uncomfortable subject for me. But Zoe just shook her head.

"I'm going to marry Chase."

"The kid who has lust for you in circle time?" Levi asked.

"Yep."

"Dude." He shook his head sadly. "Rejected by both the Sutcliffe sisters. This is devastating."

"Good thing you have Amber Janson to keep you company," I said.

He didn't take the bait. "Good thing," he agreed with a smug smile.

The next day I marched into anatomy and physiology with my head held high, determined to accept Adam's invitation to homecoming if I hadn't already completely ruined everything and sent him screaming in the direction of a cheerleader.

Nothing was resolved with the portal. Levi knew why it was there but he didn't really know how to close it, and it's not like I had any clue. Given the disturbing incident with Tyler and Levi's conviction that I was "taken" already, I had more courage than usual—which was, generally speaking, none—when I plunked my books down on the lab table next to Adam.

Going to a dance with him, regardless of why he asked me, suddenly seemed way less disturbing/frightening/important than the idea of mating. For life.

Adam was already sitting in his seat and he didn't even glance up, which would have bothered me, except that was standard for Adam.

"Hi," I said brightly, borrowing from my acting reserves and using a Perky Coed Number One voice.

Clearly startled, since I didn't usually assault him with cheerful, he shot a wary look at me. "Hey."

Then he surprised me right back by adding, "Sorry I couldn't call you back last night, but it was like ten when I got home, and I wasn't sure if your parents would freak."

Wow. That was quite a lengthy sentence. I was so proud of both of us that I actually gave a genuine smile. "That's okay. I just called to say I'm sorry for being so weird yesterday . . . but I was kind of offended to think that you invited me to the dance because Levi made you do it."

Might as well get it all out there. It was highly likely Adam would say something that wasn't going to feel all that wonderful, but it was better to know the reality. Truly. No matter how brutal it could be.

But, fortunately for my self-esteem, he shook his head and frowned at me. "Hey, I don't do anything just because someone else told me to."

Okay, that was hot. He sounded arrogant and just a little bit annoyed.

"And I asked you because I want to go with you." His eyes locked with mine, and did I just imagine it or did his gaze drop to my mouth? "I think you're . . . interesting."

My breath caught and I was suddenly very aware that his leg was right next to mine. "Okay, then. I would love to go with you." Because I was interesting. So take that, Amber Janson!

"Cool," he said.

"Yeah," I agreed.

"What are you doing Saturday? Wanna hang out?"

He didn't even want to wait until the following weekend for

the dance? We were going to have a pre-dance date? Totally amazing. Though I suspected my heart was going to need defibrillation, I started to nod a big yes, yes, yes. Then I grimaced. "Oh, wait. I can't. I have an audition for a play . . . *A Midsummer Night's Dream.*"

"Shakespeare?" he asked.

Hello. He knew my William. It was more than I could have ever hoped for. "Yes. I want to play Titania."

"Maybe after the audition we can go out . . . celebrate, you know. Because I'm sure you'll do fantastic. You have that . . ."

Adam kept talking but I couldn't understand him because our teacher was suddenly shouting for attention and making statements about passing homework in, and his freight-train voice rolled right over Adam's. I strained to hear, but there was nothing but moving lips and garbled words. Mr. Beckner stopped talking.

". . . about you."

Adam finished, and I stared at him, cursing my sucky lip-reading skills.

He had probably just given me a compliment and I'd missed it. I am completely realistic. I wasn't expecting Byronic poetry from Adam. It wasn't in his jock genetic makeup. This might be the most I'd ever get, and I had freaking missed it. It was A Moment and I got nothing. "Thanks," I said with a smile because it was too ridiculous to ask him to repeat it.

Our teacher popped up in front of us like a deranged jack-in-the-box. "Do I need to make some seat changes?" he asked.

What kind of question is that? Why do teachers do that? To answer "Yes, I think you should move my seat" would be an admission of guilt, but also an agreement to move from the person you were speaking to, and I would assume if you're speaking to them, you're friends or whatever and don't necessarily want to take chances sitting next to someone else who might not be your friend and/or might have body odor. If you said, "No, I don't think you should move my seat," you're opening yourself up for a massive lecture about the rudeness of speaking while the teacher is teaching.

No way to win, I said nothing, staring silently at Mr. Beckner. Adam did the same thing.

"No more chatting," he told us sternly. "Neither one of you can afford to not pay attention in class."

Whatever. I had a B. That worked for me.

The teacher turned around and went to the front of the room and I prepared to be bored. A second later a piece of paper slid across the desk.

Ur cell #? it said in Adam's masculine chicken scratch. I briefly wondered why guy handwriting is sort of slash and scrawl, while girl handwriting is loopy and exuberant. Or at least his and mine were. Opposites. Yin and yang.

I wrote down my number and passed it back. He tucked it in his pocket.

And when I chanced a glance at him, he smiled at me.

Yes.

Chapter Eight

I was so high on life that when Isabella dropped me off at home it didn't register that the usual female entourage surrounding Levi was missing. He was actually standing in the driveway with my dad, who had his short-term travel suitcase sitting on the driveway in front of him.

"I can't believe he's going to homecoming with Amber," Isabella said sadly as she parked the car behind my dad's Honda to let me out. She was staring at Levi with an expression of complete longing.

Feeling bad, I gathered up my backpack from the floor. I didn't want Isabella to go with Levi, because honestly, she deserved better, but it sucked that no one had asked her. She could have asked someone, but she was too stuck on the completely bizarre conviction that she liked Levi.

"He's an idiot," I said. "Asking Amber is proof of that."

"Maybe Amber isn't so bad," Isabella said glumly. "There must be something awesome about her that he likes. Either that or there's something wrong with me."

"That's blasphemy, Iz, so just knock it off. So you're not his type. Big flipping whoop." It wasn't like her to be so caught up on a guy—that was my specialty—and I was getting worried. "Maybe Adam has a friend you could go with."

She snorted, tossing back her long black hair. "I don't want a pity date. Think about how you felt when you thought Levi made Adam ask you."

"Yeah, and you told me guys need persuading sometimes. That they don't know what's right for them until you stick it in their faces."

"That was different because you like Adam. You're not sticking me in some strange soccer player's face."

"So who do you like? Just ask somebody, even as friends. I want to go with you." It suddenly occurred to me that not only would my best friend be at home, pining over my demon, but I might have to go exclusively with Adam's friends and their dates, which would be like falling into *Bring It On*. Somehow I doubted I had a whole lot in common with soccer girlfriends.

"Just forget it, Kenzie. I don't want to go."

When Isabella got stubborn like that, I knew it was time to just let it go for a while. "Okay, but call me later."

"Sure."

Her wave was half-hearted as I got out of the car. My dad was loading his suitcase into the trunk of his Honda.

"Kenzie, I'm going to New York," he said, sticking his hands in his dress-pants pockets.

"Okay. Have a good flight." My dad does some kind of obscure computer thing that requires him to fly all over the planet on a random and frequent basis. It seemed like a pretty cool gig to me. He got to pop in and out of town, eat dinner in trendy restaurants, and swoop into client sites and save the day with his computer geek skills. If I were inclined to go corporate, which I'm totally not, I'd take that route. On the other hand, it really seemed to me like my mom's life sucked. She spent all day with nasty criminals (she usually referred to them as scumbags or vermin), fighting the system to put or keep them in prison (while wearing very unflattering and boring business suits), then came home and had to do the whole dinner/chauffer/cleaning thing.

But she hadn't run off to be a Vegas lounge singer yet, so I guess she was cool with it all.

My dad kissed my forehead. "Levi is taking me to the airport, so he can keep my car. He agreed to work with you on your driving skills while I'm gone. It stresses your mother too much to go out with you."

Excuse me? The demon who had a fake driver's license was

being granted permission to drive my dad's car with no restrictions for three days? And I couldn't imagine what skills I was supposed to learn from him other than lying and teaching five-year-olds to broker higher allowances.

"I know how to drive!" I said, totally offended. Hadn't I explained to everyone—at least seven times—that it wasn't my fault that I failed? Apparently eight was needed. "It's not my fault I didn't pass. I told you that lady had it out for me. She took me into this really awful neighborhood and there were all these guys hanging around on street corners making inappropriate gestures. So I drove a little over the limit in order to preserve my safety. You didn't want me to risk my safety, did you?"

Dad frowned. "Boys were making inappropriate gestures?"

"Yes!" Hadn't he heard this story the first seven times? Or maybe I had never actually mentioned the rude gestures to my parents. Clearly that had been a mistake, because Dad looked infuriated.

"They shouldn't be driving you through areas like that. What are they thinking? I'll call and complain when I get home."

Yay, good Daddy. "So you think they'll change my Fail to Pass?" I asked hopefully.

But Dad just scoffed. "Dream on, Kenzie. You're going to have to retake the test. That doesn't mean I'm not going to complain though."

Great. "The point is I don't need Levi to teach me how to drive."

"Just tool around with him. No big deal. You could use the practice before your next test."

Then, with a squeeze of my shoulder, Dad got into the car. Levi gave me a grin and a wicked wink as he climbed into the passenger side.

"Okay, so gas is on the right, brake is on the left."

"I hate you," I told Levi as I sat behind the wheel, listening to him patronizing me.

"Wow, it's been like almost a whole week since you said that. I was starting to miss your hatred."

Adjusting the radio and the mirror, I checked out my reflection. Lip gloss gone. Good thing we were only driving to the grocery store to get milk and mozzarella cheese for my mother.

"I've just assumed it was understood that I can't stand you. But that comment called for overt hatred."

"Big words, Kenzie. Is Adam helping to expand your vocabulary?"

I put the car into reverse and gunned it. "You're so hilarious." We hit the bottom of the driveway a little harder than was necessary, but I was feeling impatient with Levi. "But maybe you shouldn't quit your demon day job and do stand-up just yet."

"So are you going to the dance with Adam or what?"

"I'm going with him." And just the thought made me feel a

little fizzy inside. Like a soft drink had gone up my nose, but in a good way.

"Huh."

"What's that supposed to mean? You're the one who told Adam to invite me in the first place." I flew down the cul-de-sac at forty miles an hour.

"Yeah, I did." Levi bit his fingernail. "So, I think tonight we should try to close the portal."

Total subject change. Slamming on the brakes when the car in front of me took too long to roll to a stop, I glanced over at him. "That would be nice. But the question still remains—how exactly do we do that?"

"I'm working on it."

"Well, that clears it right up." I took the right turn a little too hard and jumped the curb.

"You know, has it occurred to you that you didn't pass your driver's test because you're a crap driver?" Levi asked casually.

"I'm not a crap driver. Why would you say that?"

"Maybe the fact that you're on the neighbor's lawn right now?"

A glance in my rearview mirror confirmed this. "Just the back right wheel by like two inches. It happens." I adjusted the steering wheel and gave it some gas. Maybe more than was strictly necessary. Both of our heads snapped back.

Levi grabbed the door like I was endangering him. "Pull over. I'm driving."

"No!" Tossing my hair out of my eyes, I stared at the road.

"Everyone has their own style behind the wheel. Just because I'm not granny-driving doesn't mean I suck at it."

He snorted. "It means you can't pass your test."

"I told you, that's not why I failed." But we were at the grocery store, and I wanted ice cream, which took precedence over arguing with him, so I let it drop.

We had a cart full of ice cream, mozzarella cheese, milk, and whipped cream, when I heard a familiar voice say, "Hi, Levi."

Ugh. I turned around and found myself face-to-face with Amber Janson. She was wearing a tiny miniskirt with a gigantic gold belt and an even tinier T-shirt, and her blond hair was up and artfully tumbling around her face. "Oh, hi, Kenzie," she added, the smile falling off her face.

"Hey." I didn't even try to fake a smile.

"Hey, Amber." Levi gave her a warm smile and took her hand into his.

Like I needed or wanted to see that. Part of me hoped she'd smack him down in the dirt and put him in his place, but she totally let me down by snuggling up against his chest.

"What are you guys doing?" she asked, peering into our cart. "Hello, someone likes dairy."

"Yes, I love it," I told her brightly. "I eat ice cream practically every day."

"Kenzie never gains weight," Levi added. "High metabolism."

He was so getting ten bucks for that. Amber's face froze. "How lucky for you. The only thing that saves me is that I'm athletic."

Was gossiping a sport? "I can't imagine you have to worry about it," I said, actually meaning it. I had a hard time picturing Amber starving herself, and she didn't need to. She really was in great shape, I had to give her that.

She didn't answer, but petted Levi and whispered something to him.

Feeling about as welcome as mold on Mom's mozzarella, but not wanting to stand there indefinitely while they had a flirt session, I said, "What are you here for?" And how soon was she leaving?

Amber only had her keys in her one free hand. No basket or cart. She waved her hand around. "I was thinking about applying for a job here as a cashier."

No clue why someone who got everything she ever wanted would need a job, I just said, "Oh. Well, I hope you get it."

"Thanks."

My cell phone vibrated in my hoodie pocket. I grabbed it and read my text message. *U busy?* From Adam. Whoo-hoo.

No, I typed. Just dawdling in the grocery store while Levi and Amber made bizarre mating faces at each other. But that was too long to relay on a cell phone.

I hv math hmwk.

Sorry.

As gleeful as I felt, it occurred to me not for the first time how utterly boring text messages can be, and they were way more time consuming than actually verbalizing that same thought. My mouth moves much faster than my fingers.

Call me? I asked, figuring screw my pride. We were never going to get past *hey, what's up* comments unless we actually talked.

Ok.

Unable to hide a grin, I looked up and rudely interrupted Levi and Amber. "Are we done because we probably need to get home."

"Why? Is Adam going to IM pictures of himself to you and you want to rush home to drool?"

"Adam who?" Amber asked, frowning a little, probably because something social had occurred and she wasn't aware of it.

"Adam Birmingham. He and Kenzie are hooking up."

"We're just going to homecoming," I said quickly, worried somehow it would get back to Adam that I thought we were way more than we were.

"You and Adam Birmingham?" Amber's eyes were wide and disbelieving. "What in the world do you two have in common?"

Who knew? But it was frankly none of her business.

My phone rang.

An hour and a half later I had Amber's answer. We had nothing in common. Absolutely nothing. Music, movies, food, clothes—we were about as far apart as Australia and New York before the invention of flying or the Internet. And he was Australia and I was New York, just in case you were wondering, because he had that whole athletic/outdoorsy/sun-tanned thing going on, and I was thin and wore black. So it all made sense, and yes, Amber Janson was actually right about something and I was willing to admit it.

Because the thing is, it didn't really matter. Even though we didn't see anything the same way, we never had those awkward pauses in conversation, we never made each other uncomfortable, and Adam had this really unexpected and sly sense of humor that killed me, and he seemed to think I was smart and intriguing. What more could I ask for?

Well, okay, I could ask for sonnets on my beauty, but really, he'd butcher them when delivering, and I would probably get embarrassed anyway, because while I do okay, it's not like I'm destined for *America's Top Model*.

Then utter and abject devotion would be good in theory, but I don't think a puppy-dog kind of guy would appeal to me either over the long term because they always want attention, and tend to jump on you when you enter the room.

If I got a guy who shared all of my interests, right down to Broadway musicals, there was a very strong possibility he would be gay, and I already had plenty of gay male friends. I really didn't need a gay boyfriend too.

Not that I should mention the word boyfriend. *Waaay* too early for that.

But it was a really, really, very cool, funny, entertaining conversation that had me giddy and almost unaware of Levi's harassment.

Almost.

When he hit me on the head with a soccer ball, I was slammed into awareness of his presence.

I had gone onto the deck, despite the freezing October nighttime temps—at least freezing to me because I'm a complete winter wimp—and was sitting on the steps talking to Adam while Levi kicked the ball around in the backyard.

Not really paying attention to him or his occasional comments and eye rolls, I was deep into delivering a *Secret Garden* monologue to prove to Adam I could rock a British accent, when I got clocked with Levi's soccer ball. The phone went flying out of my hand and I saw stars behind my eyes. The pain burst out from the back of my skull and I let out a startled cry, tears popping up and streaming down my cheeks.

"Kenzie, are you okay?" Levi jogged over.

Did I look okay? I was sprawled across the deck, nose running, and embarrassing little sobs coming out as I fought for control over the pain. It felt like my brain had imploded, and I was suddenly absolutely certain Levi had done it on purpose to interrupt my conversation with Adam.

Trying to sit up, I felt around for the phone, wincing as my head throbbed and my hands shook. I felt like I was going to throw up and I dangled my face over the corner of the steps, aiming for the grass.

Levi picked up my phone and said, "Dude, Kenzie can't talk anymore. She took a soccer ball in the face."

And then he hung up. Just hung up! "Call him back and tell him I'm okay and that I'll call him later," I managed, wiping at my cheeks as the rolling sensation in my stomach quieted. I decided I wasn't going to puke after all.

"You're not okay." Levi squatted down and stared into my face, looking concerned. "Holy crap, I'm so sorry. That ball was flying . . . demon speed, you know. It's a miracle it didn't knock you out cold."

"Is that what you were trying to do?" I asked, taking a deep, shuddering breath and collapsing back on the cold deck.

"It was an accident. I would never do that on purpose, Kenzie." His hand kept coming out like he wanted to touch me, hovering in front of my face and making me dizzy.

Finally I smacked it weakly. "Stop it, you're making me sick."

"Sorry. Sorry." His hand dropped and he squeezed his lips together. "I'm going to go get your mom. We should take you to the ER."

"For getting beaned with a ball?" I tried to scoff, but the motion sent my stomach back up into my throat, and I rolled to my side and splattered the deck with remnants of Mom's homemade pizza.

Nasty.

Then the world tilted again as Levi reached over and scooped me into his arms like I was Zoe's size. Sliding the back door open with his foot, he told me, "Just close your eyes."

He was warm and hard and that seemed like a good idea.

With a sigh, I settled against my demon and tried to ignore the pounding in my head.

"You're such a klutz," he said. It didn't surprise or annoy me. Guys have a tendency to joke when anything even remotely serious happens.

"Call me Grace," I murmured.

Levi didn't answer. But I could hear his sigh. Feel the tension in his arms and shoulders.

He was worried about me.

Good. He deserved it.

Chapter Nine

"She's always had a hard head," my mom commented as we got home three hours later. The diagnosis was a mild concussion, no fractured bones.

"That's not funny, Mrs. S," Levi said. "I could have really hurt her." He was biting his fingernails, a sure sign he was agitated.

He and Brandon were watching TV, Zoe nowhere to be seen, most likely already in bed. Mom had taken me to the ER for X-rays and I was exhausted, but I asked Levi, "Did you make that call I asked you to make?"

I would have called Adam myself, but despite her flippant words, my mother had been glued to my side since the second Levi had brought me into the house. There was no way I was calling Adam back with my mother sitting there listening. My head already throbbed, I didn't need a cross examination from Kathy Sutcliffe, Esquire, on my relationship with Adam.

Levi rolled his eyes. "Yes."

"What did he say?" I asked, before I could stop myself. Did I really want to know? And more to the point, did I want to hear it front of my brother and my mother?

But Levi just shrugged. "He hopes you're okay."

"Who?" my mom asked.

"I have a horrible headache," I said, heading for the stairs, avoiding everyone's eyes. "I'm going to bed." Bed was the best place for me, even if my mind was racing.

My mom glanced at her watch. "Yikes. You two need to turn that off and head up too. It's eleven. We're all going to be zombies in the morning. Or at least I will. I'm sure all of you will be fine."

She shook her head, and I anticipated a "youth wasted on the young" speech, so I took the stairs two at a time, regretting it when the movement made me a little nauseous. Wondering if I should be offended that apparently Adam hadn't gushed concern, I stopped to kick off my ballet flats with the metal studs.

I jumped when Levi touched my arm. "What?"

"We need to talk."

"In the morning."

"No, now. It's about the portal."

"Is it going to explode? Did you see someone come out of it?"

"No, I want to talk about closing it."

"Then that can wait until the morning."

"No, it can't." He was so close to me that I sort of bounced off of him when I tried to move through my bedroom door.

I stopped and sighed, gathering my strength to beat the crap out of him.

"I realized something," he said.

"Wow. Stop the presses." On the verge of some serious whining, I tried to push around him. His arm blocked me. "Levi . . . please. I want to go to sleep. Why do you do this to me like every night? And after practically knocking me into orbit with a soccer ball, the least you can do is leave me to sleep in peace. Can you understand that? Just leave me alone."

That was probably more exasperated than whiny, but I hoped he would take the very loud hint and Go Away.

Suddenly he pulled his arms away from me. His eyes cooled. "Fine. We'll talk about it later. Good night."

As I watched him walk down the hall, I wondered why my victory felt so hollow.

Then I decided it had to be the head injury, because why exactly was I feeling like I was the one who had done something wrong?

Demon trick.

It had to be.

I did not actually like him. And I had done nothing wrong. Everything was his fault, his doing, his problem. Not mine.

So there.

*　*　*

But a lousy night's sleep didn't remove all shades of my bizarre guilt, and as I heard Levi leave my bathroom in the morning, I forced myself to sit up. Apparently a concussion had warranted a legit sick day—my mother hadn't even attempted to wake me up—but for some vicious and cruel reason, I had actually woken up at six-thirty anyway.

Maybe it was guilt for snapping at Levi, maybe it was fear that he seemed so urgent to close the portal (what did he know that I didn't?), or maybe it was residual brain trauma, but once awake, I couldn't get back to sleep. I wrapped a blanket around myself and went in search of Levi before he left for school.

He and Brandon were at the kitchen island, spooning huge quantities of Raisin Bran into their mouths. My brother raised an eyebrow. "Nice hair."

A glimpse at my reflection in the microwave showed that somehow during the night my hair had become lopsided, a huge cotton candy kind of lump rising above my left ear. Whatever. I tried to run my fingers through and got my nail caught.

Dragging the blanket behind me, I leaned against the island.

"Are you feeling okay?" Levi asked. "Should you even be out of bed?"

"I'm fine." Despite having a bad hair day, my headache was gone. I was tired from having my mother wake me up in the middle of the night to check my lucidity, per the doctor's orders, but I was hanging in there. It was touching to know he cared though.

"You look like hell."

Jerk. So much for my guilt. "Thanks to you."

"Dude, it was an accident, I swear. I would never hurt you on purpose, K."

"Okay, fine. Accidents happen. I'm not mad at you. Much. So let's talk about what you wanted to talk about last night."

"That's kind of like a private conversation," he said, tilting his head toward Brandon.

My brother grimaced. "Okay, if you two are going to get sexual or something, I'm outta here."

I rolled my eyes. "Hardly. Eat your cereal and be quiet."

"She saves that for Adam Birmingham."

My stand-up comedian was back. "What is it about Adam that bugs you so much?"

"Nothing bugs me about him. He's cool. We're friends, we hang out at practice. He's just not your type."

"What is my type?" And why did that sound like such an insult coming from him? I knew Adam wasn't really my type, I knew I didn't know a thing about soccer or football or baseball, but who said anyone had to have a type? Who said you had to only hang out with or date someone who was a social clone of yourself?

"Someone more like you," Levi said. "Someone, you know . . ." He waved his arms up and down in front of me to indicate my appearance.

"Someone with bad hair?" Brandon asked.

Levi laughed. Pushing myself off the island, I pulled my blanket tighter around me and shuffled back toward the stairs. "Never mind. This conversation is going nowhere, much like all of our so-called conversations."

I stomped up the stairs and defiantly went into my bathroom. I missed my bathroom. My own space. My towels. My little glittery soap dispenser, and my Hello Kitty Dixie cups. I resented that Levi was using my bathroom, and was jealous that he had walked into my high school and a minute later had created a life for himself. He fit in. Instantly. And while I didn't want to be a slave to fashion, trends, or a small-minded sheep mentality, I couldn't help but want to fit in. Just a little. With *some* crowd.

Glancing in the mirror, I decided it wasn't ever going to happen. Yikes, look at the hair. Might as well accept reality. Debating whether to return to bed or to head down the hall to the other bathroom for a shower, I capped the toothpaste Levi had left lying out.

"Kenzie."

A faint whisper hissing near my ear had me dropping the toothpaste into the sink. That was not the voice of anyone I knew. I whirled around. There was nothing there. "Okay," I said out loud. "I'm losing it."

Which, frankly, was better than the alternative—that there was a demon in my bathroom. A different demon. The demon I didn't know as opposed to the demon I did know.

"Help me." This time the voice was clearly coming from the shower and it sounded like a woman. Her pleading tone sent shivers up and down my spine.

Whatever help she needed, I was sure I was the wrong person to ask. I couldn't even pass my driver's test, there was no way I was going to be able to assist a supernatural being. That portal needed to go away, and I should have forced myself to have the conversation about it when Levi had been willing. Frozen in front of the mirror, I debated running, screaming, or both simultaneously.

"Please . . . help me, Kenzie. It hurts."

Okay, load on the guilt. I glanced over at the shower. No one was behind it. Not physically. Whoever was speaking was still in the portal, because the shower curtain wasn't rustling, and there was no feeling of another person in the room with me. That made it way less scary, and she was knocking on the door of my conscience with her desperate whispering.

The voice sounded so pitiful, so frightened. She gave a pain-filled cough, like she'd just been kicked in the ribs or something. The sounds were horrible, like listening to a catfight outside and wanting to help, knowing you can't or shouldn't.

Sliding the curtain back slowly, I held my breath, anticipating another bloody face in my drain. It was a face. But instead of an evil, blood-splattered, gelatinous mass, I saw a girl about my age. She had a gorgeous, satin-white face, heartbreakingly beautiful as she cried in agony. The tears rolled down her face like glossy pearls.

Leaning in for a better look, I whispered, "Who are you?"

There was a rushing roar in my ears and I suddenly felt like I was falling, like time and space had disappeared and I was under water, floating in warmth. The face sharpened, the tears glistened, the eyes beckoned, the mouth lifted in a welcoming smile, and I felt . . . important. Like my presence mattered to her happiness.

But before I could smile at her or say anything, I was suddenly yanked out of the tub, stumbling backward three feet until I collided with the sink.

"Are you insane? What are you doing?"

That voice, I knew.

I blinked at Levi, confused. "I don't know." My heart was racing and I felt sad, like I'd been denied something wonderful, yet at the same time I was scared. Whatever had just happened, I suspected it wasn't cool. "What?" I glanced toward the tub, wanting to see, wanting to know who or what that was.

Levi stepped between me and the tub, his hands on my shoulders, holding me back. "Don't look."

"Who was that?" I tried to look around Levi's head. I couldn't help myself. My palms were sweaty and my foot tapped impatiently as I waited for his answer.

Levi grabbed both of my cheeks and forced me to lock eyes with him. "Do not look. It's a prison guard trying to pull you into the portal."

"A prison guard? Are you sure it wasn't a prisoner?" That

wasn't my image of a guard. On TV, they always have bad skin, short hair, mirrored sunglasses, and a really cranky look on their faces, which totally makes sense given the fact that they spend their days with violent criminals who resent authority. This girl did not look like any prison guard I'd ever seen, and I could have sworn she was no older than eighteen.

"No, it was definitely a guard. Water prison. Their talent is to reflect your needs and wants back on to you, like seeing yourself in water. It establishes your trust, makes you content in their presence so you don't riot or attempt escape."

"I have no reason to riot or attempt escape. I'm not a prisoner." And what exactly did a whining, crying, beautiful girl have to do with my needs and wants? I felt confused all over again. "Why were you in water prison anyway?"

"I told you why I was in prison."

"But what does a water prison mean?"

"Let's go into your room," Levi said, still holding my face. "I'll try to explain everything."

"No," I said, suddenly feeling stubborn and tired of the whole thing. "I want answers to everything. Right now. And stop squeezing my cheeks. It makes me feel like you're my aunt Becky." It also made him really close to me, and that wasn't helping my equilibrium. Somehow when I got in front of him, all the pieces that didn't seem to fit together when I looked at Levi from a distance seemed to work individually. He had a strong jaw, nice lips, white teeth, and dark eyes with flecks of gold.

It was unnerving to look at him and think he was attractive.

"Okay," he said, dropping his hands. "Okay, fine, but you're not going to like what I have to say."

I just stared at him, folding my arms across my chest. He was going to be late for school if he didn't hurry up. Not that the secretary would mark him tardy. He had her wrapped around his finger too, like everyone else in my world.

"Remember that the prisons are built on the points of the pentagram? Well, each is ascribed to an element—mine was the element of water. We're water demons, I guess you could say."

"Water demons. Like water snakes?" It was so hard to keep up with the underworld creatures, considering I hadn't even known they'd existed two weeks earlier. "And I thought you were an envy demon."

"I'm both. It's sort of like origin versus occupation."

"Okay, I think I have that." Freaky and disturbing as that was, I did actually think I had a handle on it. "So how important is water to you? I mean, is it hard for you to exist here without it?"

"No. Water just enhances our power. That's why the portal is in the shower. But the thing you really need to understand, Kenzie, is that the prison guards will try to pull you into the portal—that's what both of those demons were trying to do. They really, really want you."

"Why do they want me?" I should have been paralyzed with fear at the idea of being a demon Twinkie, but truthfully, I was curious. I couldn't imagine what I could offer to a demon, unless they wanted to be entertained with a monologue or my rendition of "All That Jazz."

"They want your energy, your mortal essence."

"Well, they can't have it."

"Which is why you need to close this portal."

It always came back to that. "Why do I have to do it?"

"Because you opened it. That's the only thing that makes sense. You open it, you have to close it."

"Except I don't know how." He just seemed to conveniently forget that little part on a regular and annoying basis. "And if I close it, that means you are here permanently, right?"

"Possibly."

Loved how he was noncommittal when he knew I wouldn't like the answer. "We have some serious issues to work out. One: You can't live here forever. My parents are going to spot the gaping holes in your black-mold story soon, and eventually at school they will figure out you have no guardians when no one shows for parent-teacher conferences." I stuck my fingers up in the air. "Two: We have both managed to ignore that little 'find a new source of sustenance' on our To-Do List, and I know, know for a fact, that you are just running around creating huge quantities of envy in half the people in my school. I'm sure all the guys on the soccer team are totally jealous of you just walking onto the field and being the new star, and every girl you smile at wants to impale every other girl you smile at. Three: You're ruining my life. Before you, I never had underworld demons pawing me in the front seat of their Chevy Impalas, or trying to suck me into the bathtub drain."

"You also never had a date with Adam Birmingham before."

He just had to throw that in my face. "Adam and I would have hooked up on our own eventually."

Levi snorted. "Sure, whatever. But none of this matters, because the reality is that you need to close that portal if you don't want to die, and I'm not going back. So you're going to be here, and I'm going to be here. The rest are just details we can work out along the way."

Details. Just details. "Okay, since you just know everything, tell me how to close the portal."

Was that a grimace? Of course it was. Because he didn't know how to close the stupid, stinking portal, so the entire conversation we were having was completely and utterly useless, as usual.

"Maybe I should explain."

"That would be a start."

"This area is a center of paranormal activity. . . . It's geographically located so that it's exempt from most natural disasters. It has a core energy from its elevation and proximity to water. It was the site of Indian and early white settlers' spiritualism. But most importantly, it sits right on top of the correctional system of the underworld."

"So basically I live in the suburb from hell? And yet it's always so boring here."

"Sarcasm isn't necessary."

"So what does correctional system mean? Prisons? Reform schools for wayward demons who suffer guilt and give the candy back to the kid they've stolen it from?" The sarcasm continued to roll out. I couldn't help it. It was either that or fall on the floor in a puddle of hysteria, and since Levi had been using my bathroom, I doubted the cleanliness of the ceramic tile.

He ignored my little witticism. "Yes, prison. The five prisons form a pentagram right below West Shore. Each point in the pentagram of the individual prisons has a portal, like we talked about. This portal," he gestured behind him, "is open. Bad enough. But if all five portals ever opened at the same time, then the entire pentagram becomes a portal that opens up . . . so all of West Shore becomes a portal connecting the underworld to the mortal world."

Whoa. "So, that means . . ."

"That anything down there can come up here. All at once."

"Yikes." I could feel my face go hot.

"And just so you know, I suspect that you were born a demon slayer."

Dude.

Chapter Ten

A demon slayer. Me? That was a complete and total joke.

"Okay, let's recap here, Levi. I cannot possibly be a demon slayer. I can barely walk across the room without tripping. I don't have an athletic bone in my body and I've never touched a weapon in my life. I don't watch supernatural-type TV shows, and I have bad reflexes. I failed the Presidential Fitness Test in school, and Zoe could probably bench press more than me. Not to mention I don't own any leather outfits or know any banishing spells. Plus I don't have a driver's license." I have no idea what not passing the BMV test had to do with anything, but it seemed important to list it along with my other Couldn't Possibly Be a Slayer attributes, or lack thereof.

But his jaw was set and his arms were crossed over his chest. Somehow our legs had both come apart, and we were facing off like gunslingers. Or toddlers fighting over a donut. Or a teenage girl and her demon pal. Which was the most ridiculous? I could hardly wrap my head around it.

"It's the only thing that makes sense. You were immune to Tyler."

"I thought that was because I was 'taken,'" I said, still profoundly disturbed by that.

"True. But you opened the portal. And twice you've resisted going into it."

"Because you were with me both times." No matter what he said, I was going to have a rebuttal, because I absolutely refused to be a demon slayer. I wasn't one, and no one could make me.

"That soccer ball to the head should have killed you. I kicked with full strength."

"You heard my mom. I have a hard head. When I was a kid I had bunk beds, and when I was about seven I fell out of the top bunk when I was sleeping. Not only didn't I crack my head open, I never even woke up."

"Kenzie, sooner or later you're going to have to consider that it could be possible. You might be a slayer."

"Don't you have to be born to slayer parents to be a slayer?" The only thing my dad took down was wayward mail message programs.

"Your mom is a slayer. She puts criminals in jail, men who are truly evil."

A shiver raced down my spine. I'd never thought of mom's career in that way before. But Levi was right. Mom slayed the very real dragons. Or demons.

"I don't want to be a slayer." Which sounded really whiny. But come on. Demon. Slayer. Didn't that just sound completely frightening? I couldn't even make it through a haunted house without having a panic attack, and those were actors with fake blood. What would I do when faced with a real, in the flesh, demonic creature?

Apparently I housed them in my brother's room and got driving lessons from them.

Sometimes it was so hard to remember that Levi was a demon.

"I mean, if I haven't killed you yet, what makes you think I have it in me to drop a really evil dude? Besides, those faces in the bathtub weren't tangible, they were just puddles of goop. How do you fight that? Not to mention that I don't know how to fight anything—I've never been in a fistfight. Isabella has, back in seventh grade with the new girl who started spreading rumors that Iz was pregnant—in the seventh grade, can you stand it? But I don't think she could help me with this either."

I paused for breath, thoughts scattered.

"Are you done babbling?" he asked.

"No. I don't think I am." I wet my lips. "Levi, the bottom line here is I refuse to be a demon slayer. I wasn't born one, I didn't sign up to be one, and I won't be one."

"Levi, are you upstairs?"

That was my mom's voice.

"Yes, Mrs. S," he called out around me.

"You're going to be late, sweetie. You'd better hurry."

Sweetie? That was just so wrong.

"Okay, I'm on my way." He put his hands back on my shoulders. "Relax. We'll talk about this later. In the meantime, stay out of this bathroom. I'm serious. Do not set foot in here without me."

Like I had to program that into my PDA. Please. I wasn't going near that tub anytime soon, with or without him. Getting sucked into a prison portal didn't sound like a good time, really. I'd willingly subject myself to an eighties perm before I dove into that mess.

"I'm just going to hang out in my room. I might even come to school for a half day so I don't miss my American lit test."

"I'd never forgive myself if something happened to you," he said.

Then he leaned forward and kissed my forehead.

Right as my mother knocked on the door. "Levi, it's time to go!"

Good to hear she didn't nag me and me alone.

But that still didn't distract me from my confusion over the lip contact. So it wasn't a real kiss. Just a forehead touch. Sort of like an arm squeeze. But it still felt strange and not at all brotherly or friendly. It felt almost guy/girl, and that completely freaked me out.

So I didn't say anything at all, just stood there in my pajamas and bedhead like a total freak—yeah, big surprise—and watched him move around me and open the door.

Which really was just stupid on his part.

My mother's face went from concern and mild irritation to primal rage. "Why are you locked in the bathroom together? In your pajamas?"

"Uh . . ." What legit cover could I pull out of my butt in two seconds? None, apparently.

"We were discussing how to close a demon portal," Levi said as he slipped past her with a smile.

The truth sounded insane out loud, so it was actually a good strategy. I was impressed.

Mom not so much. She frowned. "You two may think this is cute and funny, but I'm serious. I don't want you closing yourselves up in rooms together."

"It's a bathroom, Mom," I said, annoyed at her implication. "What do you think we could be doing in here?"

"The fact that you can't imagine all the things that could occur in a bathroom reassures me."

Eew. What did she mean by that? Mental imagery of her and dad doing *all the things that could occur* in the bathroom sort of slammed into my imagination before I forcibly banished it. I so didn't want to go there.

"But still, no closed doors." She did the finger thing and I fought the urgent need to roll my eyes.

"How is the mold removal coming along?" My mom turned and asked Levi.

I shot him a *See?* look. There was no way he was going to be able to stay more than another week or two without my parents starting to question who he belonged to and why they'd never actually spoken to his alleged parents.

"It's real bad," he told her as they started down the steps.

"Take it easy today!" My mom threatened me over her shoulder.

Once they were out of sight, I headed down the hall for a shower, then went straight to my computer. There was no Webster's definition for demon slayer, but it wasn't hard to figure out.

Demon: an evil spirit.

Slayer: a killer.

Demon slayer, therefore, would be one who kills evil spirits.

Yeah, like that was going to happen.

I used Google to look up "demonology," and spent an hour looking at pictures of winged naked creatures with unpronounceable names like Azazel and Beelzebub, which sounded like someone's redneck uncle. According to various online encyclopedias and websites, demons seemed to be, well, evil spirits, out to convince humans that doing wrong was seriously cool. No mention of how to deal with them.

I was just grateful Levi had shown up in my tub in jeans and a T-shirt, given some of the images and drawings online. They always seemed to be hovering maliciously over a long-haired, well-endowed woman, who opened her ruby-red lips in surrender. One picture in particular had me studying it closely. The girl was gorgeous, with milky white skin, flushed cheeks, auburn hair, and bright blue eyes. The demon was ugly with a capital *U*. He had bumps all over his face, big lips, glowing yellow eyes, gigantic, scaly wings, a bulbous butt, and long toenails.

Yet she was half dressed and clearly about to give it up to him. Which was just insane. What woman in her right mind would fall for that pock-faced mess? I didn't get it.

Then suddenly it occurred to me that maybe what that chick was seeing was some dapper dude in eighteenth-century breeches and buckle shoes. Maybe she was looking up at her fantasy come to life, hot brooding eyes, sexy hair and all, precisely so she would fall for him. Maybe that's why Levi had shown up in my tub wearing jeans and a T-shirt.

Not that Levi was my fantasy, because if I were clicking to buy, I would have ordered him with ears that didn't stick out, and broader shoulders. And he wasn't a lust demon, after all. He was Envy.

Which I'd been feeling plenty of, hadn't I? I was green with envy for his social success, and for his driver's license.

Had he shown up in a nonthreatening form just to manipulate me? To use me as access to my school and friends?

Not a pleasant thought.

He had never exactly told me how he had wound up in prison, or how exactly it was him who popped through the portal and not someone else. It made me wonder why I had never asked. Maybe because I didn't really want to know the answer. It was easier to sit back and pretend he was just a normal guy who appeared in a slightly unusual way.

Who told me I was supposed to be a demon slayer. And that I'd met my mate.

The question was, how much of what Levi said should I believe, if anything?

I needed to test him. The question was how to do it.

The situation called for Pop-Tarts, so I headed downstairs, hoping for brilliance over a sugar-laden breakfast.

While processed sugar and carbohydrates are generally inspiring, I didn't like the path they led my brain down.

As I chewed, I figured I had three options for discovering if Levi was legit and telling me the truth.

1. I could try to kill him, for real, and see if he went evil on me.
2. I could tell him I accepted my role as slayer and ask him to mentor me.

3. I could ask him how to close the portal (I just knew he knew how to do it).

All three options pretty much sucked. The first, while appealing in theory—considering all the trouble Levi had caused me, really wasn't in me. I don't like to stomp spiders, and though he could get on my last nerve, I couldn't see myself stabbing or shooting or poisoning Levi—by the way, no clue here how to get my hands on a big knife, a gun, or poison. This would require research and a toughening of my inner self, along with the eradication of all human compassion.

Not a nice-girl choice.

The second wasn't as bad. I could fake actual interest in being a demon slayer. I was an actress, after all. Highly trained and all that. But the thing was, at what point did I say, "Oh, hey, guess what, I really don't want to be a slayer? Sorry for wasting your training time." If he was being honest and up front with me, chances were it would really irritate him that I was lying like a rug.

Number three sounded iffy, but I was definitely leaning toward it. After all, if his suggestion to close the portal worked, I would have to assume he was telling the truth, right? And I wanted the portal closed, that was a given. So it would be accomplishing two goals at once, and I was all for multitasking.

Door number three worked for me.

*　*　*

What I discovered three days later was that it isn't easy to drop that into idle conversation. *So, how about that portal?* Levi had already told me he didn't know how to close it. He had been pretty straightforward about that. Before, I had thought he was trying to give me that demon-slayer line to make it my problem, since he said he didn't know how to close the portal, but now I was wondering. What were his motives? Would it benefit or hurt him if I was a slayer? And why wouldn't a demon himself know how to close a portal?

Something stank, and it wasn't my brother, Brandon.

And I still didn't know how to get to the truth.

Tossing off random statements like, "You know, if I poured that zit cream down the drain again, what do you think would happen?" didn't get me far.

"I don't know," he had replied as we were driving to the mall. Levi needed a suit for homecoming and I needed a dress.

It had occurred to me that it was incredibly weird that we were shopping together for formal wear, but I didn't want to ask Isabella because she was acting annoyed with the whole homecoming issue. Most of my other friends who ranked high enough to go shopping with were my theater friends, and they were more into thrift shops than chain stores. And while I'm all for a bargain, something about wearing a previously worn dress to homecoming wasn't appealing.

"I guess you could try dumping your zit cream and see what happens." He grabbed the dashboard. "Slow down. I want to get to the mall in one piece."

Easing off the gas, I said, "You don't sound real into trying different ways to close this stupid thing. I thought you were worried about my safety. If you were really worried, you would help me think of ways to close it."

He shrugged. "I just don't think that will work."

Which convinced me he knew it wouldn't work. Because he knew what would work. But wouldn't tell me.

It was a problem.

As was the fact that every dress in the mall looked like a six-year-old beauty pageant poof of bubblegum pink, yellow, or sky blue, or was a straight sheath in glamorous colors like emerald and burnt sienna, which would be fab on one of the *Desperate Housewives* cast members on Emmy night but was way too old for me.

There had to be a happy medium somewhere, only the middle seemed to be missing in half of the overexposed dresses that screamed clubbing and pimp shopping.

Levi held up yet another Cinderella dress. "What about this one?" He seemed determined to cover me in layers of chiffon.

"Since I don't think Adam will be picking me up in a pumpkin stagecoach, I'll pass, thanks."

Shoving it back on the rack, he sighed. "You're too picky. It took me five minutes to find something. What's the big deal?

Adam's going to look at your dress and be picturing you out of it anyway. Trust me, he's not going to care what the dress looks like."

"You're disgustingly crude." It was an automatic response, but my heart wasn't really in it as I yanked dress after dress across the sales rack. Nothing. I was starting to get nervous. I really didn't want to wear a glorified tutu.

"I'm a guy." But that didn't stop him from selecting another dress, this one a vivid plum color that would clash with my red hair tips. "What about—"

"No."

"Come on, you'd look pretty in this one."

Sure, if I were auditioning for *Charlie and the Chocolate Factory*. "If it says glitter on the label, I probably don't want it." What I wanted was a dress that reflected my personality. Apparently my needs weren't first and foremost on homecoming dress designers' minds, because there was *nothing*.

Two hours and six stores later, I would have felt sorry for Levi if I wasn't so frustrated. I couldn't find anything that I liked, or if I liked it, they didn't have my size, or I looked like a number two pencil in it. My It dress didn't seem to exist.

Levi was alternating between groaning and singing White Stripes lyrics to himself. He had laid out completely on a bench outside the fitting room and was staring up at the ceiling, holding his stomach.

"Come on, Kenzie, just pick something. *Anything*. This is worse than prison. At least they didn't starve me there."

"I told you to go get something to eat. I don't care." I was hot and in a bad mood, and I stuck my head—with hair rising from static cling—out of the door. "Can you get me this in the next size down?"

It was an okay dress, black lace with a regretful pink sash, but I figured I could ignore that for the sake of wearing something on my body, or better still, I could dye my hair tips pink to match. I was desperate.

Still lying down, Levi stuck his hand out and grabbed the dress. It fell on his face. "So am I supposed to go eat after I get this in the next size?"

"Sure."

He peeled himself off the bench. "You do know Adam Birmingham is not worth this."

"Get the dress!" I was standing there in my cami and jeans, which I'd been forced to pull back on so I could open the door, not to mention I always find it weird to stand around a fitting room in bra and panties waiting for a different size. It smacks too much of a visit to the doctor. But I was getting tired of pulling my clothes on and off and standing barefoot on dirty carpeting.

A really long and boring five minutes later, he reappeared. "I couldn't find that dress, but the saleslady had this one in the back. She said it's new, very trendy." He held it out, a doubtful look on his face. "I don't know. It looks kind of weird to me, like a funeral shroud or something. But with an Austin Powers kind of vibe."

That sounded promising.

Three minutes later, I knew it was the It dress. It was sheer black with a straight skirt and vertical satin stripes to give it a subtle shimmer. The neckline was square, with shoulder straps, and altogether it managed to work. It was short and very chic, and it made my scrawny legs look like an asset. I felt sleek and cool in it, yet not like I was wearing a forty-year-old's dress. Just odd enough to be me, yet classy.

Taking a deep breath, I smoothed the material over my stomach, and opened the door. "What do you think? I kind of like this one."

Levi turned and I had the satisfaction of seeing his mouth fall open. "Dude," he said.

I thought that was a good dude, but I wasn't sure. "Does it look okay on me?"

Sure it did, I was also positive he would shrug or scoff or make some crack about giraffe legs.

But he just shook his head slowly and stared at me. "You look . . ." His voice was a little tight, and I sucked in a breath. "Amazing. That is totally a Kenzie dress."

Aah. What a guy. Demon. What a demon. Unable to stop it, a grin spread over my face and I turned around, feeling happy,

happy, happy. I was right to hold out for the perfect dress. I really liked the admiration I saw on his face, and it pleased me that he got it, what the importance of the dress was to me. "Thanks, Levi."

"Now can we go eat?" he asked, face screwed up in agony again. Apparently thirty seconds was all I was capable of diverting his attention from his stomach.

"Sure. We just have to hang all these back up." I handed him a giant pile of multicolored fabrics and miscellaneous hangers with a big smile. "Thanks. I'll get changed."

"This is retribution for the soccer-ball thing, isn't it?"

"Would I do that?" I slammed the door shut.

If he had ulterior motives and was playing me for a demon fool, I figured I might as well make him work for it.

Chapter Eleven

How Not to Question a Demon, by Kenzie A. Sutcliffe.

First and foremost, avoid anything that might be controversial. Pretend all is going to go away. Live in denial. And dance around the subject endlessly while demon stuffs face with massive burritos.

"Um, I guess we should do something? You know, about the situation . . ."

Shrug from Levi.

"So, hydrochloric acid, huh?" I thought that might spark something.

Nod.

"Maybe you could show me those calculations or whatever they were."

Noncommittal eyebrow lift.

Hey, I tried. But I don't like confrontation.

So if you totally don't want to accomplish anything in a questioning session with demon otherworldly entities, simply go home and fixate on upcoming date with soccer-star lab partner who has been giving you really cute smiles when he sees you at school.

It's what I did.

And then I went on my date with studly soccer-star lab partner and completely forgot that I had a demon living with me who claimed I had some higher purpose that involved slaying evil beings.

On same said date, all I cared about was making sure I didn't come across as a freak—which I probably am, but why scare Adam immediately? Of course, he already was witness to a certain level of freakiness when I questioned his homecoming motives, and he was still hanging in there with me.

My audition went okay—I don't think I was brilliant, but I didn't totally suck either. Admittedly I was distracted. And I took a little flack from my friends when Adam picked me up at the theater in his Lexus SUV and strolled into the lobby wearing clothes that screamed *I'm an Athlete.*

"He's so not your type," Sara said under her breath.

Lindsey gawked. "Whoa. Hard body."

That made my cheeks go hot, which I completely despise. Blushing should be illegal, and as far as I can tell—though I am in science for dummies—there was no biological explanation for why my face went pink and splotchy on random occasions when I was embarrassed.

Jamie made little *"mmm, mmm,"* sounds. "You go, girl. What playing field did you pluck him off of?"

"Do not follow me," I hissed to them as I started forward. Adam was looking a little intimidated at approaching me while I was ensnared in a pack of over-pierced, massively accessorized females.

"Hi," he said with a nervous smile.

"Hey." I smiled back. Then realized my friends were right behind me when Adam's eyes went wide.

"I want to know if your intentions toward Kenzie are honorable," Lindsey demanded.

"And what time you're going to have our little girl home," Jamie added.

Without looking I could just tell she had her hands on her hips and had gone into the role of Protective Mother, Stage Left.

"And if you have—" Sara started.

"Bye!" I yelled, and startled Adam by grabbing his hand and yanking him toward the door. "Love you guys. See you Monday."

Moving fast, I tripped over the doorjamb, and didn't even

pause to reflect on how embarrassing that was. What was be-hind me was much, much worse. A stern tug on Adam's hand had him stumbling behind me until we were in the parking lot. "Where's your car?" I demanded.

"Right there." He pointed to the Lexus right in front of my face.

Duh. Hadn't I just seen him get out of it when I'd been rub-bernecking out the window watching for him? Fear made me stupid.

Adam opened the door for me. I vaulted in, yanked the door shut, and locked it.

When he got in the driver's side, he glanced over at me and frowned. "I wasn't going to do anything to embarrass you."

"What?" I chanced a glance back at the theater. My friends were waving and making faces. "What do you mean?"

"You didn't have to drag me from your friends like that. I know you think I'm kind of a dumb jock, and maybe I am, but I wasn't gonna like scratch myself in front of them or any-thing."

Didn't see that coming. I was so worried that my friends would humiliate me by insulting Adam that I didn't realize he might get the wrong idea and be insulted anyway—by me. How cool to know he had insecurities too.

At that moment, I lost all the nervousness I'd ever felt with Adam. I grinned—part from relief, part from the image of him clawing at the front of his jeans. *So* not an Adam thing to do. "I didn't think you were going to scratch yourself. I was terrified they were going to say something bizarre and embarrass me. I was trying to protect you from them."

"What would they say?" he asked, looking a little relieved, but not totally convinced.

"Something designed to torment me. But trust me, I don't think you're a dumb jock." I thought he was a really, really cute jock. With a touching sensitivity. "Where are we going?"

"You hungry? We could get some dinner."

"I'm always hungry," I assured him. No sense in playing the anorexic with him. He'd find out soon enough that I love food, especially when it's going into my mouth on a consistent and frequent basis.

"Cool." He glanced over at me as he started the SUV. "What are you smiling about?"

I bit my lip to try to contain my grin. "Don't mind me. I'm just a freak."

Adam grinned back. "I like that about you."

Five hours later we concluded that he liked a lot of things about me, including my lips.

After pulling into my driveway to drop me off, Adam moved in for a kiss, and I was game. We'd had a great time going to dinner and the movies, and he was just a good guy. Skilled with the snogging too. One kiss turned into two, which turned into time to say good-bye before Dad glanced out and saw fogged-up windows.

"You have beautiful eyes," Adam said after we broke apart for air.

"They match my hair," I told him, feeling like I'd had helium injected into my chest. I was floating high on endorphins and some serious like.

He laughed. "That was a stupid thing to say that day, wasn't it?"

"Nothing is stupid when it's a compliment."

Clearing his throat, Adam looked away, drumming his fingers on the steering wheel. "Can I tell you something?"

"Sure," I said, my giddy bubble popping immediately. That didn't sound good. That sounded like a preface to a confession that he was dating me only to get close to Levi, or that he had realized he was busy cleaning out his closet the night of homecoming and could no longer go with me.

But he looked back at me. "I knew who you were," he said in a low voice. "I've known all year who you were."

"Oh." That was good. That was really good. I could ask him why he had pretended not to know, but I wasn't sure he would actually answer with the truth, and I figured I knew why anyway. Maybe Adam had been crushing a little bit himself. And if he hadn't been, it was much better to assume that he had.

Besides, he was clearly into me now as he leaned forward, intent on picking up where our lips had left off two minutes earlier.

Unfortunately, I almost fell out of the car when the door was yanked open, letting in a blast of cold October air. I heard Levi's voice, in a scenario that was oddly familiar, except this time I was perfectly content to be getting a little attention, unlike when Tyler had creeped out on me. I was also one hundred percent certain Adam was not a demon.

"Hey, guys, what's up?" Levi said in a very friendly voice.

Adam stared over at him in disbelief. I turned and shot him an evil glare.

"Go back in the house," I said, with no attempt to be subtle.

"Only with you." He gave a sweet smile—I hated when he could look so innocent—and took my hand in his. "Mr. S says it's time to head in for the night."

"I'll be there in two minutes." I tried to extract my hand, but Levi had clamped down on it.

"Nope. You're coming now." Levi tugged me so hard, I either had to come with him or spill out onto the driveway. "We'll catch you later, Birmingham."

In a blur, he had me in the house. It happened so fast, my feet tripping over themselves, that I suspected he had turned on a little demon speed.

"What do you think you're doing?" I demanded as we went in through the garage door to the kitchen. "I didn't even get to say good-bye, and how rude is that?" A quick glance around confirmed that my parents were already in bed and had actually taken no part in his chaperone role-playing.

"Just saving you from yourself and your soccer stud's hormones."

"I don't need to be saved, thank you very much." And even if I did, where did he get off presuming to be the one to save me?

"Could of fooled me."

"It wouldn't be hard to fool you," I retorted.

"What is your problem?"

"You. You're my problem."

"Your problem is that you're throwing yourself at Adam because you're jealous of girls like Amber who always have a guy."

Hello. Where did he pull that convoluted logic from? There were so many things wrong with that, I didn't know where to start. "I am not jealous of Amber." Not much, anyway.

"Are you kidding me?" Levi laughed. "Honey, I've been feeding off of your envy for two weeks. Trust me, you are jealous."

I felt the blood drain from my face. "You've been feeding off of me? That is absolutely disgusting." And I was not jealous. Much.

"Well, I can't help it . . . it's just there. It would be like wasting a perfectly good brownie by pitching it into the trash. If there was a brownie being waved under your nose, you'd eat it, wouldn't you?"

No clue what to say to that, and feeling strangely mortified, I grasped for another argument. "I am not throwing myself at

Adam. We're hanging out. It's none of your freaking business, Levi."

"Hey." He held his arms out. "You want to screw up your life, fine. Go for it."

"The only thing screwing up my life is you." I was so angry, I was starting to shake, and tears popped up into my eyes. Wasn't I allowed to have something good happen without everyone criticizing me and trying to take it away? And how could he just eat at my expense? It felt violating, and I wondered if he had dated Amber on purpose, just to irritate me. To make me envious. To feed.

Levi said something under his breath, shaking his head.

"What?"

"Nothing."

Exasperated and feeling a little sick to my stomach, I tossed my coat on the kitchen island and ran up the stairs.

"Keep it down," he hissed after me. "You'll wake up Zoe."

Like he cared about my baby sister more than *me*.

Leave it to me to unlock the most self-righteous demon in hell.

Levi and I seemed to not to be speaking to each other the rest of that week. Or at least I wasn't speaking to him. And after a few days he gave up trying to talk to me.

Portal or no portal, I really felt like I couldn't just let him run around making my choices for me, and I thought he owed me a serious apology for eating on my dime.

Apparently he didn't agree, so rather than argue for the seventy-third time, we just avoided each other.

But I was busy enough with the rest of my life that I almost didn't miss his grating presence.

Monday, we got our interims and Adam and I were both getting Cs in A&P. Mr. Beckner split us up and saddled me with Eric Dobson, who had a mucus issue that required him to make wet sounds in the back of his throat and nose at five-second intervals. Adam came over to study that night and to commiserate over our new seating arrangements, as he had gotten Samantha Schwartz, who had a tendency to burst into tears for no apparent reason. While I was disgusted by Eric, Adam was terrified he'd send Samantha into a suicidal spiral if he didn't toe the line in their dissections.

Tuesday, I found out I got a part in *A Midsummer Night's Dream*, though only a supporting role instead of a lead, which sort of sucked.

Wednesday, flowers showed up at my house—an assortment of wildflowers with a congratulations card from Adam for getting a part. Can you stand it? What guy is smart enough to not get roses or something completely weird like carnations, and to say congrats instead of sorry? Bonus points for Adam.

Thursday, Adam suggested I could wear his away game football jersey to the homecoming game Friday night. Whoa.

And Friday, I did. It was surreal, maybe rushing things a little, and totally way out of character for me to show up at a football game decked out in athletic wear. Actually, it was strange for me to even attend the game, but the fact that I did, and enjoyed it, showed how far I had fallen for Adam.

I mean, there I was, wearing a black turtleneck that I'd had to borrow from Isabella, a white number seventeen jersey that said *Birmingham* across the back, and my jeans rolled up so you could see my one black, one white soccer socks that I'd borrowed from my brother. I'd even tossed on some black and silver beads to go with the outfit, and a black hair ribbon. Then I'd panicked because I looked too not me, so I added a black studded belt to keep it real. Plus I'd changed the ends of my hair from burgundy to hot pink for homecoming, which I thought went really well with the black and silver school colors.

My dad actually did a double take when I came down the stairs. "Where are you going?" he asked.

"To the football game." Maybe he thought I was hitting a Halloween party. That was probably more reasonable for me than what I was actually doing.

"Oh." A tortilla chip in his hand, he paused with it halfway to his mouth. "Where did you get that football jersey?"

"Adam Birmingham. He's the placekicker. At least I think he is. He's the guy who kicks the ball between the goalposts when you're not close enough to get a touchdown." I stuck my fingers up like tiny goalposts to illustrate my point.

My poor father looked entirely perplexed and it wasn't from my lack of football knowledge. "Well, why do *you* have it? Doesn't he need to wear it in the game?"

"This is his away game jersey."

"So, why . . ."

"Because they're dating, Bill," my mother finally said, breaking through the fog for Dad. "That's why."

"Oh." The chip went in his mouth. "A football player?" he said, crunching as he spoke. "Not Levi? I thought . . ."

"That's the problem, babe," my mom said. "Don't think. Just go with it." She kissed my dad on the cheek as she breezed past him, stealing a chip from his bowl.

Exactly. Just go with it. That's what I was doing.

And I actually had a good time at the game, even if Isabella whined about the cold the entire time, and even if I got grilled by half a dozen catty girls as to why I was wearing Adam's jersey.

"Where did you get this?" Nikki Williams said, plucking at my sleeve as she went by me on her way to the designated homecoming court section of the stands.

"I stole it," I told her. "I could probably get you one, too. What number do you like?"

She rolled her eyes. "You're a total freak."

"That's true," I said, cheerfully.

"Hey, Nikki, can you keep moving?" Amber Janson said. "I have vertigo and standing here makes me sick."

Nikki started moving farther up the steps, and I checked out Amber and Levi as they came into view. Amber did look a little panicked, and she was clutching the center railing like she would levitate without it. I felt downright sorry for her.

"Don't worry, I'll catch you," Levi said, which somehow eradicated all my sympathy in a microsecond.

They were dressed up, since they were both on the homecoming court—yes, I know, not even a month in my school and he had wormed his way into the King's Court—and Levi had his hand on the small of Amber's back.

Whatever. I turned my attention back to the football field. There were lots of guys out there, and they were all moving around. That was about the most I could figure out. Finer points of the game were lost on me.

"Nice jersey," Levi said to me.

"Thanks." I faked a smile his way, then pretended like I really knew what I was watching.

"Isn't that Birmingham's?" Tim Gable said from right behind Levi, two steps down from where I was sitting. The question wasn't directed at me, but at Levi.

"Yeah."

Tim was a short, stocky wrestler with more brawn than brain. He glanced over at me and shook his head. Then he said to Levi, as if I couldn't hear every word he was saying, "Damn, how many times did she have to do him to get that? Birmingham's weird about his clothes."

Nice. My cheeks flushed with anger, but I was prepared to ignore him. It would just make a big scene if I protested, and he wouldn't believe my denials anyway.

Apparently Levi didn't agree with my "let it be" philosophy.

"What did you say?" he asked, turning slowly to Tim.

Tim laughed, not catching the tone in Levi's voice. However, I knew that particular expression, and his body language was screaming trouble to me. When Levi got quiet and stiff like that, he was highly annoyed. I opened my mouth to interrupt, but Tim punched Levi in the arm jokingly and said, "You heard me. A girl like that is only good for one thing."

Levi didn't even bother to answer. He just shot his fist out and nailed Tim in the nose. Amber screamed, both because his sudden movement had her dangling off balance on the steps, and because Tim's nose had burst on impact, blood streaming down over his lips.

"What the hell?" Tim demanded, grabbing at his face.

"Levi, don't worry about it," I said, trying to scramble over Isabella's legs to get to them. I couldn't believe he had just punched Tim Gable. He was a trash-talker, everyone knew that. It wasn't worth bloodshed. Iz keep tugging on me, trying to hold me back, and we wound up sort of piled on top of each other, a tangle of denim and hair.

"Don't talk about Kenzie like that," Levi said.

"I'll say anything I want about her." Tim moved closer, getting in Levi's face. "And what are you sticking up for her for, anyway? She doing you too?"

That was the end of it. Levi went at him, and they both fell sideways onto the bench, scattering game viewers and a box of nachos with cheese. Amber screamed like the devil's helpmate was after her—which he wasn't, he was punching out Tim—and clung to the railing like she was on the *Titanic* and it was going down. I almost laughed, but didn't want to waste the time as I concentrated on getting off the bench and across the aisle.

It was ludicrous. Clearly I wasn't destined to sit and watch football. A couple of dads were debating breaking it up or letting them pummel each other until they worked it out. Levi had Tim's face on the metal bench and was saying, "Take it back."

"No way," Tim answered, cheek compressed. Even in that awkward position he radiated attitude, and with a sharp kick he nailed Levi in the calf.

I used to think it would be sort of cool to have a guy fighting to defend my honor, but in reality I was waffling between embarrassment and the need to giggle. And I was starting to worry that the cops—who hung out on the track and near the concession stand—would be appearing at any given second.

So when they both stood up and faced each other, obviously ready for round two of Macho Man, I did a really stupid thing. I moved in between them. Which was exactly when Tim went in with a right hook meant for Levi's face.

Since I was standing on the bench, I was higher than Levi and the blow landed on my shoulder, knocking me completely off balance, teeth rattling and brain jarring. That was the second time I'd gone down, only this time Levi caught me, and we hit the bleachers hard. If Levi hadn't been on the bottom, I probably would have cracked my skull open, but his demonic bones took the blow, and I only had the wind knocked out of me, and scraped my hand brutally along the concrete.

I blinked, feeling like my lungs had collapsed, as Levi groaned. "Ow. That hurt. You okay, Kenzie?"

"Fine." Arms hauled me up from overhead.

It was Tim, dusting me off, concern all over his face. "Sorry, sorry, I didn't mean to hit you. Are you okay?" He rubbed my shoulder vigorously, right where he'd punched me, and I fought the urge to wince. It was actually really sore, but I didn't have the heart to tell him he was hurting me even more. I just tried to shift away, not wanting to get his blood on me either. The bleeding from his nose had slowed down, but he had blood splattered all over the front of him. Not a good look, and I was wearing a white jersey.

"I'm fine."

"Get your hands off of her," Levi said, hauling himself off the ground and glaring viciously at Tim.

"You're not finished, Athan? Come on then. Try to take another piece of me." Tim held his hands out in a taunting gesture.

That was it. I rolled my eyes. "Okay, just knock it off." I put my hand on Levi's chest to stop him from charging Tim again. "Levi, thanks for sticking up for me, but it is not worth getting suspended over, okay? Now go help Amber up the stairs. She's trapped and having a panic attack. And you," I pointed at Tim. "If you feel the childish need to call me a slut again, why don't you just go and write it on the bathroom wall? It would save us all a lot of trouble. Now I'm going to sit down and watch this game."

Which was a good thing, because the cops were making their way up the steps as I spoke. Isabella pulled me back across the aisle with a hissed, "Get over here, Kenzie," and I went willingly.

Tim gave me a sheepish look. "Hey, sorry."

Sure. But I was willing to be big about it. "Okay."

Levi ran up the stairs to Amber, and we all tried hard to look innocent. The blood on Tim's face sort of gave him away, but he claimed he had tripped going up the stairs and had fallen down, taking Levi and me with him, but that we were all okay. No one seemed inclined to dispute the story, and that was that.

Except I had managed to get Tim's blood on the shoulder of Adam's football jersey after all, I had a sore shoulder, and a hand that looked like I'd taken a cheese grater to it.

Go West Shore.

Chapter Twelve

Leaving my room when I heard the doorbell ring the next night, I almost bumped into Levi, who was wearing the suit I'd helped him pick out.

"Excuse me," I said. Frosty had nothing on me. While I appreciated the fact that he had wanted to stick up for me with Tim, I didn't appreciate that he had done it in such a public way. And I was still hurt and confused that he had used my envy, maybe even stoked it, to feed himself.

"Hey, wait," he said, grabbing my arm when I would have gone down the stairs.

I turned back, impatient, but figuring we might as well have our argument before my parents let Adam in.

"I want—"

Levi abruptly stopped speaking and looked up at me. "Whoa. Even better with the shoes. You look like you strolled off a catwalk, K."

Flattery would get him halfway there. I thawed a little. "Thanks. Now I have to go." I could hear my dad opening the door and greeting Adam.

"I know. And I hope you have a good time with Adam. Seriously." He looked me straight in the eye. "But first I want to tell you about the portal."

"What about it?"

"You are a slayer, Kenzie. And I know you've been trying to get me to tell you how to close the portal. The truth is, I know how, but I can't tell you. It's impossible. All I can do is hint. So the thing is, you can close the portal, I know you can, and it's important that you do it soon. It's growing."

Wonderful. I wanted to believe him, I really did. So I said, "Okay, hint then, Levi. Give me something."

"Just remember, it's a water portal. It's all in the plumbing."

Yeah, that cleared everything right up. I was hoping for like a "step A followed by B" kind of plan. That really was nothing more than a hint. I sighed. "Levi . . . I'm not a slayer. I don't know how to do this."

He took both my hands and squeezed. "Yes, you do. Stop underestimating your strength."

What strength? I almost laughed. I didn't know what to say, and I turned my head toward the stairs, hearing my father making small talk with Adam—a crack about girls never being ready on time.

"Okay." Levi let go of me. "Have fun with Adam. But be careful. And remember what I told you."

Plumbing. Sure. But for some reason, I paused. "Do you really like Amber?" I asked quietly, not even sure why I cared.

He just looked at me. Then said, "There's more to Amber than you think, K."

I nodded. Maybe he was right. "You guys have fun too."

"My parents called tonight," Levi said.

"Excuse me? What parents?"

"My parents," he said, giving a pointed glance toward the stairs. "They talked to your mom and explained that they're getting a divorce, and it looks to be ugly. They asked if I could stay here for a few months."

How the hell had he managed that kind of conversation?

"But I told Mrs. S. we needed to make sure it was cool with you."

I wasn't sure why it was, but I said, "Yeah, it's okay," without really any hesitation.

"Thanks." He squeezed my hand. "Now go downstairs before Adam sweats his way through his suit."

"See you at the dance," I said, and went down the stairs, unnerved by what I was feeling. Anger had made sense to me, but this strange sort of confusion didn't. I should have sent Levi packing without a backward glance, but I hadn't.

I didn't even understand myself, how could I expect anyone else to?

Everyone stopped talking and stared at me when I hit the bottom of the steps. Way to make me feel comfortable. I stood there and gave Adam a nervous smile.

He was gaping at me. I took it as a good sign.

Mom teared up, doing that hand over her mouth thing that means she's going to ball and launch into a "you were just a baby yesterday" speech.

But my dad beat her to it with a "Jesus Christ."

"Bill!" my mother blurted in shock.

"Kenzie, you need to go upstairs and change. That dress isn't even decent."

Was he joking? "Dad! This dress has sleeves! It doesn't cling to me. It has a neck. You have lost your mind." And was mortifying me in the process.

"Bill." My mom smacked him on the arm. "You're embarrassing her. And she's not showing an inch of skin."

I wasn't. I had on black tights and Mary Jane pumps. "We're leaving," I said, my cheeks probably the color of my hot pink hair tips. "Sorry my dad is insane, Adam. Let's go."

My dad jumped up off the couch. "Sorry, K. It's just you look so . . . mature."

Exhibit A: Father ruining his daughter's social life. If he mentioned my breasts, I was going to slit my wrists.

My mom said, "Have fun. Be home by curfew." She shot me a look, waving her hand in an indication that I should get out before Dad went off the deep end.

I grabbed Adam's hand, which had my dad making a choking sort of sound in the back of his throat, and I rushed the front door. When we were outside, I said, "Oh my God, I'm so sorry. That was just weird. My dad is such a—"

Whatever I was going to say was cut off by Adam's mouth on mine. Oh. Didn't see that coming. But I was liking it nonetheless.

"You look gorgeous," Adam breathed, his mouth still close to mine. "I really, really like this dress."

I did too. And I really, really liked the way he kissed me when I was wearing the dress.

Unfortunately, his mother hated my dress almost as much as my dad did. Or maybe she just hated me.

Either way, it was obvious Mrs. Birmingham was mourning the fact that her son was the only one without a blonde in a pink dress at his side. Both Adam's friends, Justin and Reggie, met us at his house for pictures with their dates, Darla and Madison.

Apparently various mothers had been invited as well, and it was something of a cheese and wine occasion for the adults as they posed us in seventy-two combinations. Then checked the digital shots to see if they came out. Then retook the ones they weren't satisfied with.

But given the pained and embarrassed looks Mrs. Birmingham kept giving me, my hair, my dress, my shoes, it was obvious Adam hadn't warned his mother that I don't artificially tan and I'm not a perky five foot one. She made at least three references to my height:

"Goodness, you are so . . . statuesque."

"Better put Kenzie in the middle of Darla and Madison because she's so much taller."

"Maybe you could bend your knees, dear, so we don't throw the picture off balance or cut your head off."

Yeah, seriously. I was going to do it, just to keep the peace, but Adam glared at his mother.

"Mom! She doesn't have to bend her knees." He turned to Darla's mother. "Mrs. Baldwin, can you take one that's longways of me and Kenzie? I want all of her in a shot."

"Sure, sweetie." Mrs. Baldwin was at least three glasses of wine into that bottle of red, and she was flushed in the cheeks and clearly feeling accommodating.

Adam pulled me tight up against him and grinned down at me. "Smile."

I did. And Mrs. Birmingham looked like she'd swallowed her cracker with brie whole.

Even though I had trouble differentiating between the two of them, Darla and Madison were actually very sweet to me. They kept touching my dress and saying how much they liked it.

"I'm way too short for that," Madison said.

"And I've got way too much in the hips," Darla added. "I would look like an inflatable pool raft. But you look hot, Kenzie."

"Thanks. I like your dress too. I can't wear pink."

"Just in your hair," Mrs. Birmingham muttered.

I figured at that point Adam and I were even. My dad and his mom . . . it was a toss-up who needed a bigger gag.

Adam reached out and tugged the pink tip of my hair. "I think you look good in pink."

Oh, yeah, his mom hated me.

But Adam didn't.

And that was good enough for me.

Okay, you know how you always imagine the way an event will play out in your head and it never, ever goes the way you pictured? Even when you create at least six different scenarios? That happened with homecoming.

I expected that Adam and I would have a decent time, but that I would feel uncomfortable around his friends, and that somehow word would get to Adam about Levi and Tim's little confrontation in the bleachers the night before.

What I didn't expect was that Darla and Madison and I would bond over bruschetta, that Justin and Reggie would treat me like I'd always been around, and that Tim Gable would serenade me with "You've Lost that Lovin' Feeling," down on his knees as his way of an apology. Someone had clearly been watching too many eighties movies through Netflix.

It seemed I was getting used to being the center of embarrassment because I could only laugh as Tim did a fair job of imitating a young Tom Cruise, though with wider shoulders. We caught quite a lot of attention, obviously, and I saw a few flashes that indicated it was likely this would end up in the yearbook, or at least on various MySpace pages. Plus it had the added benefit of making Adam even more attentive to me, like he was afraid if he looked away some random guy might just make off with me.

Levi and Amber walked past me at one point and Amber gave me a perky wave that actually looked genuine. Not sure what to make of that. So I just waved back.

Adam insisted he couldn't dance, which I found hard to believe given that he played soccer, football, and baseball. That took coordination. I begged him until he gave in, and proved that, in fact, he couldn't dance. He looked like electric shock therapy gone wrong. So he had one flaw. I had way more than that. And he was a good sport about it, pulling Darla and Madison over to dance with me when he retired from the floor, laughing.

"He likes you," Darla said in a sing-song voice as she shook it to Beyoncé.

"You think so?" I asked, pretty sure he did, but really enjoying hearing someone else say it.

"Oh, yeah," Madison said, holding up her little finger. "All you gotta do is wrap him, sweetie."

As if I had any idea how to do that. I'd have to stick with the current plan, which was just to be myself. Lame, but there it was.

"What about Justin and Reggie? Have you guys been dating for a long time?"

"Since last year," Darla said. "Things are cool. We're tight."

"Reggie and I are just friends." Madison looked a little wistful when she said that.

Darla nudged Madison, sending them both off rhythm. "Madison won't go for it, even though I tell her some guys just need you to take them by the hand and show them what's best for them."

"My friend Isabella told me the very same thing," I said. "And it was so true."

"Is that what you did with Adam?"

"Totally." Okay, so that really wasn't the whole truth, because technically he had invited me to homecoming without me actually having done anything. But I'd thought about it enough that it almost seemed like I had taken action. And I had called him. After I had told him I wasn't sure I wanted to go with him.

Who was I kidding? I didn't do anything. I had waited around for Adam to suddenly discover me, and for some weird reason it had actually worked. Madison needed to be less wimpy than I had been.

"Well, after I knew he liked me. Which was lame. You should just go for it, Madison. I mean, what if you go all year and never do anything and this whole time Reggie has liked you?" I was yelling because the music was pumping bass.

She shrugged, clearly not ready to commit to throwing herself at him.

"I think Levi gave Adam a suggestive shove toward me. Maybe we could give Reggie a shove."

Probably a bad idea, and hopelessly middle school, but I felt sorry for her. But given the sheer horror on her face, she didn't like my idea either.

"No! It's fine. We're just friends."

My dramatic inner soul was seriously hoping Reggie would overhear us, swoop down, and swing Madison into his arms like in a chick flick. That didn't happen. Big surprise.

Instead Madison said, "What's with you and Levi?"

"Nothing. We're friends. He lives with us."

"Uh-huh."

Uh-huh. That was it. Levi and I knew that, even if no one seemed to understand it. And as a matter of fact, he was doing some bump and grind thing with Amber right at that very moment that probably violated the code of conduct for school dances. No moshing, no tomfoolery, no dirty dancing, no bumping and grinding, no gathering in crowds of more than five students or doing anything that in some way might actually create physical contact with a member of the opposite sex.

Though apparently once you achieved status of king and queen—Levi and Amber—you could pretend you were in an Usher video and no one cared. If he started break-dancing between her legs and no one protested, I was going to have a serious problem with that.

Fortunately for all of us, they didn't stray from waist grabbing and hip shaking.

Not that I should care one way or the other.

Why did I care?

Except that for some strange reason, it felt like Levi should belong to me, in that he was my demon, my friend, living in my house, and guarding my bathroom. And no one knew.

It seemed wrong that he wasn't what everyone thought he was, and I had to lie for him, yet he was burning up the dance floor with Amber Janson.

While I felt like Morticia Addams dancing between Darla and Madison.

But I had Adam Birmingham waiting for me in the wings.

I glanced over at him, and saw he was watching us. Me. Watching me. He nodded to acknowledge that he saw me seeing him watching me.

Crush meets reality. It really was a beautiful thing.

Chapter Thirteen

When I got home from the dance—after only a brief good-night kiss from Adam because we'd gotten saddled with Madison and Reggie, who were suddenly acting completely cold and weird around each other—I kicked my shoes off and padded up the stairs. Adam had asked me out again for the next weekend. He'd even sort of hinted around that we shouldn't hang out with anyone else, meaning exclusivity.

That worked for me, and I flicked on my bathroom light and reached back to unzip my dress, happy, happy, happy with the way Adam and I were working out, and not really thinking about the fact that my bathroom was off-limits.

It was just a habit to go in there. Because before Levi had

popped into my shower, you know, I was actually able to use my bathroom on a regular basis.

But with my head full of Adam and what we might want to name our future children, should the need ever arise—I was leaning toward Devin for a girl—I forgot Levi's warnings about the portal.

Which was why I was so unprepared for my shower curtain to disintegrate before my eyes and what looked like liquid arms to reach out and grab me.

But despite being caught off guard, one hand on my dress zipper, and my head out to lunch, I instinctively dodged the touch. Whether it was territorialism for my bathroom kicking in, concern that those wet hands might ruin my very Me dress, or actual survival instinct, I have no idea, but I dropped down and followed that move with a quick scramble backward.

Screaming never occurred to me. I didn't want to wake up the whole house, and something told me Levi wasn't home yet. I was on my own, and truth be told, I was more irritated than scared. Who did these demons think they were? This was my house, my shower, my life.

They needed to back off.

The entire tub and tile had melted like marshmallow over a campfire, and my shower curtain seemed to have been sucked into oblivion. The view from up on my tiptoes by the door showed that the drain of the tub was swirling around and around in a quick, wet whirlpool. The arms that had tried to snag me were gone, but everything was shifting and moving so fast, it was hard to tell if anything was solidifying and disappearing or if it was all just a big, wet mess.

Opening the door and keeping my eye on everything, I moved out into the hall and pushed the button on the doorknob so that when I closed it the door would lock from the inside, preventing anyone from entering.

It was all in the plumbing, Levi had said.

Clicking the door shut tightly, a little surprised that nothing tried to rush me, I stared at my bathroom. All in the plumbing.

The danger of dealing with the plumbing in the bathroom was that in order to dismantle any plumbing I would have to hang out in there for a long time, disconnecting and removing pipes. First and foremost that required some kind of plumbing knowledge that I just didn't have. It also meant many, many opportunities for demonic beings to form and suck me into the underworld while my head was beneath the sink or behind the toilet. Not first on my To-Do List.

I could wait for Levi or call him on his cell phone. But in the meantime, my shower was being obliterated. Which was just rude.

Running to my room, I grabbed my cell and dialed Levi. Maybe he would have some advice. He answered, laughing, clearly still having a good old time with Amber. "What?"

"There's a small problem in my bathroom. The walls to the shower are disappearing and big wet arms tried to grab me."

His voice instantly changed. "Don't do anything. I'll be right there. Get everyone out of the house. Zoe first. Water demons like the energy of little girls."

"What?"

No chick on a liquid diet was harming a single blond hair on my baby sister's head.

"I'm on my way." Levi hung up on me. Hung up.

On my own for at least ten minutes, I had an idea. Running full throttle, flicking lights on behind me as I went, I ran for the basement, tearing down the steps two at a time. Careening to a stop at the bottom, I went for the corner that had all the faucets to turn the water on and off in the house and to the yard. I wasn't sure I knew how to do it, but I figured I would just turn them in the opposite direction of how they were at the moment and that would cut the water off to the house. The hope was that would prevent the demons from crawling up the drain, if water was them their element.

Breathing hard, I cranked all three faucets and glanced around at the pipes. All in the plumbing, right? The bathroom pipes were easy to tell apart from the ductwork because they were white and hollow, and I had heard water from the dishwasher and the shower rushing through them before. They ran along the wall to the right, coming down from the kitchen. If I was looking at it correctly, the pipes met upstairs right outside my bathroom door, and headed straight down to the kitchen, along the garage wall.

In my homecoming dress, tights, and no shoes, I went back

upstairs, checking to see if the bathroom door was still locked, which it was. Then, trying not to make a lot of noise, I opened Zoe's door and sighed in relief at the sight of her tucked up tight under her fuzzy purple comforter. She had her annoying moments—like when she had colored on my new denim skirt with marker to make it prettier—but she is my sister and I love her. Nothing would harm her while I was still standing.

So when I heard the doorknob on my bathroom door start to rattle, I dug deep for my inner demon slayer and found the answer that had been hovering around my consciousness for the last few minutes. Closing the door on my sister, I ran back down the stairs, pausing for my homecoming shoes. Hopping into them, I lifted my mom's car keys out of the kitchen bowl where she always tossed them.

Aware that I was potentially doing a really stupid thing, I opened the kitchen door, glancing at the clock glowing blue on the microwave. Three minutes to midnight. Perfect. My hand hit the button, and I sent the garage door open, hoping it didn't wake my parents up. Then again, they would probably just assume it was Levi coming home. He had my dad's car. My mom's minivan was in the garage.

If I had stopped to think, I might have found the Swiss cheese–sized holes in my grand plan. But there was no time for thinking. I had thought my way through the past sixteen years, and for once it was time to just do it. To take my own advice to Madison, and take control. No more hanging back and hoping things would work themselves out if I just waited long enough.

Beeping the door unlocked, I got in the minivan and backed it up. I was sure that the entire network of plumbing was primarily in that wall right in front of me. It was nothing more than plumbing, drywall, and a few pieces of wood. On the other side was the kitchen, so I would have to be careful.

Just a tap to disconnect. That's all. No biggie.

Unfortunately, my Mary Jane slipped on the pedal and instead of bumping the inner wall of my house with the minivan, I stomped on the gas by accident and hit the garage wall at full speed.

Oh, yeah.

I'm serious. The impact was loud and jarring, smacking me backward as air bags exploded in my face and to my left. That was when it started to occur to me that my idea wasn't exactly packed with brilliance. But the end came as quickly as the moment I lost control, and I was suddenly sitting there, uninjured, breathing hard, the front end of my mom's van in the kitchen.

Water was spraying everywhere, which gave me a certain sense of triumph. I had hit the plumbing, if those caved-in pipes to my right were any indication. Hands shaking a little, I tried to open the door, but it was stuck, so I crawled back to the sliding side door, which was still in the garage and behind the point of impact.

It was as I was struggling to open the door, my heart pounding and my fingers slippery with sweat, that I heard the most awful otherworldly screaming, and the rush of tornadolike winds all around me. When I turned to see what the heck was happening, I couldn't see anything, but I could hear the sound spiraling down the pipes where they had blistered and burst in a scattering of plastic shards. Then there was a slam, and silence.

Like a portal had closed.

The minivan door slid open, and I stumbled out, feeling pretty darn proud of myself. I had closed the stinking portal. Without help. Just me, all on my own.

Demon slayer. Yeah, baby. That was me.

Then I saw my father standing in the doorway, hands on his head, no shirt, sweatpants sliding down his hips, an expression of complete and utter disbelief on his face. "What the hell?" he asked, voice trailing off. "What am I looking at?"

"Kenzie!" my mom shrieked, sticking her head around my dad. "Are you okay?"

"I'm fine," I called, rolling my neck to work out a kink as I crossed the concrete garage floor. "I just, uh, had a little accident."

"A little accident?" My father's face turned an intriguing eggplant color. "You just drove the van into the kitchen! Oh, my God . . . How in the hell did you manage to do that?"

"Bill, it's okay," my mother said, petting his arm. "It's fine . . . Kenzie's fine. That's the important thing."

Seriously. And I had just saved my whole family from potential soul-sucking slavery in a prison portal. Didn't that count for anything?

Brandon's head appeared over the hood of the van. "Whoa." He covered his mouth like he was trying not to laugh. "Nice parking job, K."

"Kenzie?" Levi ran up the driveway behind me. "What happened? Are you okay?"

"Yep." I crossed my arms and edged toward him. "Just fine. I just had to um, drive Madison home after she and Reggie got into a fight, and well . . ." I glanced at my dad, who was now holding his chest like a heart attack was in progress. "I sneezed when I was pulling in and hit the gas instead of the brake."

That sounded pretty good. "Sorry," I added to my father, biting my lip. Then I whispered to Levi, "Go check on Zoe."

His eyes widened. "Kenzie . . . did you . . . on purpose?"

"I closed it," I said under my breath, the feeling of triumph returning. "I'm positive it's gone. But go make sure Zoe's okay."

He nodded, glancing back over at the van. "Dude."

Not exactly a thank-you, but he was probably waiting until my parents were gone to tell me how impressed he was with my quick thinking.

After Levi scooted past my parents, my dad said to me, "Where's your purse?"

"My purse? In the family room. Why?" I frowned and moved forward as my dad turned and snatched my purse off the couch.

He unzipped it and yanked out my wallet.

"What are you doing?"

Another second and he had my learner's permit in his hand. "There is no way in hell you are taking that driver's test next month. You'll be lucky if I let you take it before you're thirty."

"Dad! It was an accident." I looked to my mom for support, but she was just standing there, her lips squeezed shut.

Brandon bounced on the hood of the minivan and my mother dashed toward him. "Get off of there! For crying out loud."

"Dad!"

But my father charged into the kitchen, tossed my permit into the sink and turned on the garbage disposal. We all heard the plastic catch and grind and shred, threatening to stop the disposal. But the motor triumphed and won, making pulp out of my permit. My future freedom.

Well, that sucked. "That's a little overdramatic, don't you think?" I demanded.

"Overdramatic?" Dad flipped the switch off. His arm shot out toward the damage. "You just drove the van into the god-damn kitchen!"

"Well, technically, I didn't drive it *into* the kitchen, the front just went through the wall." Which he probably didn't care about at the moment, but I felt compelled to point it out.

"Upstairs! Now. Or so help me, Kenzie Anne . . ."

That didn't sound good. I ran. As I went up the stairs, I heard my mother say, "I guess we should call a tow truck."

"You think?" my dad answered, dripping with sarcasm.

"You know, there's no reason to get snippy with me," she said.

Great, I had my parents fighting. I paused at the top of the stairs and listened from around the corner.

"You're right, Kathy. But better I'm snippy with you than I allow myself to murder our daughter, which is what I really want to do."

Wonderful. But I could tell the heat was already going out of his voice.

And then I heard my mom whisper, "She gets her driving skills from my mother."

My dad let out a bark of laughter. "Isn't that the truth. Good Lord. Okay, why don't you go get dressed while I call the tow truck? Hopefully they can be here in an hour or two."

They went into efficient mode, ready to fix the mess I'd made. I went to find Levi. He was closing the door to Zoe's room and he gave me a thumbs-up.

"It's cool. She slept through the whole thing."

"And the portal?" I asked, glancing nervously at the bathroom door.

"Closed. Look for yourself."

The door was open and a quick pop of my head through the doorway revealed that my bathroom was completely normal. Every towel in place, except for one crumpled on the floor. The shower curtain was in place, the drain nice and shiny. It looked so normal that it took me a second to realize it was very normal. Pre-Levi normal. None of his stuff was in there. My DVD player was on the counter, my zit cream out, cap off. A wad of toilet paper was half in, half out of the garbage can.

It was exactly the way it had been when the portal opened. "How is that possible?"

He shrugged. "How is anything possible? It is."

"Why didn't you go back?" I asked, that thought occurring to me for the first time. I could have sent him back to prison without even meaning to.

"That wasn't your intention."

"No. I just wanted to protect Zoe, to have things back to normal. I wanted to make it happen, without waiting for you. I was impatient."

Levi reached out and brushed my hair back off my face. "You were strong, that's what you were. Demon slayer, I'm telling you."

His touch felt good, reassuring. But I scoffed. "No thanks. That was my one venture into slaying, and it wasn't like I actually took anything down. I just closed the portal."

"That was enough."

He was right, and I had to admit, I was proud of myself. No more waiting for someone to fix it. I had fixed it, and that was satisfying. "But what happens to you now? Are you officially free of the demon world?"

"Not exactly. I'm safe for now, thanks to you. But I still have to feed." He smiled. "And I suspect I won't be getting any more nourishment from you. Your envy seems to have evaporated. Good for you. Bad for me."

Now that he mentioned it, I was feeling pretty enlightened by my whole homecoming experience. The thing was, just like I wasn't necessarily what people thought I was, neither were they what I expected. It was time to be a little more open-minded and worry less about what other people had and more about appreciating what I did have.

"I'm sorry." Not that I wasn't envious anymore, but that there was no other way for him to feed.

He laughed. "It's cool. No shortage of envy from other people, that's for sure."

"We really need to convert you to pizza. It's a lot less immoral."

"There's a thought. But I'm not holding out much hope." A shadow crossed his face before he raised his eyebrows up and down. "So, you have fun with Adam?"

"Yeah. And you and Amber looked good out there for your royal dance. The official one."

"Thanks." He tapped his finger on my nose. "Go to bed, you wild woman. Tomorrow's going to be a long day. I suspect your dad is going to have about a million random chores for you to do."

I wrinkled my nose. He was probably right. "Lovely. Can't you pull some demon mojo on him and influence him to go easy on me?"

"That would be immoral."

"Jerk." I kicked off my shoes and bent over to pick them up. "Are your parents really getting a divorce?"

"I don't have parents."

What a concept. I shivered. Annoying as they could be, I couldn't imagine life without my family. It sounded lonely.

"You can have mine," I said lightly.

"Thanks for sharing." He waved. "Good night, K-Slay."

I rolled my eyes. "No nicknames, please."

"Sure. We don't want things uncomfortable between us when I'm chauffeuring you around everywhere since you can't drive."

On that horribly cruel note, I headed for my room and my bed. But I couldn't resist smacking him on the arm as I went past.

Grabbing my hand, he said, "Hey, K?"

"What?"

He grinned at me. "That was a very cool move with the van. I admit, I didn't see that coming. You're actually a little scary, you know, but I like it."

Despite the impending punishment, I couldn't help but grin back. "Thanks. I thought it was inspired."

And so was I. Instead of heading to bed, I decided to go downstairs and help my parents clean up the kitchen after the car was extracted.

"Bye, Kenzie."

The way he said that made me stop and look at him, heart pounding. "Are you leaving?"

But he just shook his head. "Sorry, you're stuck with me."

That really wasn't such a bad thing.

Go back to school in style
with Berkley Jam

Violet on the Runway
by Melissa Walker
As seen in *CosmoGirl!*
When a model scout whisks Violet Greenfield away from
her small town to New York City, the quiet life she knew
changes forever.

Girls That Growl
by Mari Mancusi
Third in this hip, sassy vampire series.

Queen Geeks in Love (Available November 2007)
by Laura Preble
"Give the nerd in you a chance to get up and shout" (*Girls'
Life* magazine) with the second book in this fresh series.

The Band: Finding Love (Available November 2007)
by Debra Garfinkle
Catch up with the hit band Amber Road as they navigate
their newfound fame—and their fragile emotions.

Manderley Prep: A BFF Novel (Available December 2007)
by Carol Culver
Welcome to exclusive academy Manderley Prep, where the
only thing harder than the classes is fitting in.

Go to penguin.com to order!

About the Author

Erin Lynn has had a lifelong obsession with books and other-worldly creatures, and the ability to combine both as a career makes her extremely happy. Though *Demon Envy* is her first teen novel, Erin has written thirteen bestselling novels for adults. Visit www.erinlynnbooks.com for the latest news on the DEMON series and for fun contests!